THE LIFT THAT WENT LOONY

By the same author:

I Wonder If Chocolate Kills Brain Cells
Educating Andrew
Oodles of Poodles
The Great Baked Bean Scheme

Charlie the Dog in…

The Lift
That Went
Loony

ANDREW WOODING

Phoenix

Front cover and cartoons by Mike Kazybrid

ISBN 0 85476 310 4

Phoenix is an imprint of Kingsway Publications Ltd, 1 St Anne's Road, Eastbourne, E Sussex BN21 3UN. Typeset by Nuprint Ltd, Harpenden, Herts.
Printed in Great Britain by BPCC Hazells Ltd, Aylesbury, Bucks.

For Steve and Helen Huxley.
Thanks for letting me
sleep in the 'baby' room!

Contents

Extract from *A Dog's Life: Charlie Digestives Remembered* by Harvard Naff © 2032 (used by permission of The Phoenix Publishing Empire):

It may seem hard to believe now, but there was one point in Charlie the Dog's long and varied career where he was seriously considering packing it all in.

Yes, Charlie the Dog, who had already triumphed over Evil Egbert, the mutant school swot who forced the entire world population into sweating over hours of geography homework because he hated everyone so much. Those he hated the most he would assign dull history essays to as well, along with the memorisation of log tables. Ugh.

Charlie the Dog, who had brought to justice The Massive Big Thing That's Black and Yucky, a radioactive lump of tar from Ipswich. The Massive Big Thing That's Black and Yucky would say 'Tar very much!' before splatting its victims with smelly tar, and that was why Charlie brought it to justice. There was nothing he hated more than super-baddies who told awful jokes.

Charlie the Dog, who had foiled the plans of the

Fear Brigade, a nasty trio of intergalactic space pirates who planned to take over the whole of the Milky Way galaxy using the world's supply of baked beans. (He had also uncovered the secret behind the legendary Loch Ness Monster in the process.)

Yes, Charlie the Dog, who had scored all of these victories and more (and would continue being victorious in the future), was actually wondering whether he'd done the right thing by becoming a detective in the first place. Amazing, but true.

What exactly caused all this soul-searching? And what eventually happened to make him change his mind?

It's a long story, but then this is a long official biography, so I might as well tell you the whole thing.

And the best place to start, I reckon, is a café in London in the early 1990s....

(Note to the reader: the following story carries on from *Oodles of Poodles* and *The Great Baked Bean Scheme*, the first two books in the Charlie the Dog series. Also, for some of our overseas readers, 'lift' equals 'elevator'. Got it? Good.)

1

The Real World

It was business as usual at Greasy Joe's Caff in Tooting. Eggs were on the boil, chips were being deep-fried, sausages were sizzling in their pans, and grease, grease, and yet more grease, was stuffing the stomachs of all of Joe's customers who just couldn't get enough of it.

All of Joe's customers, that is, except for a highly depressed poodle detective, sitting alone in a secluded corner of the café. He stared out of the front window while ignoring all the persistently cheerful music blaring out of Joe's cheap ghetto blaster. Unusually for him, this poodle didn't have a single item of food in front of him. He wasn't in the mood for eating.

'What's-a-matter, Charlie?' enquired Joe, wiping yucky egg yolk onto his greasy apron while handing Charlie a mug of extra-strong tea. Joe lit up another cigarette—his twentieth that day—and added: 'Why ya look so down? Un-Happy Hour eesn't-a for a few more minutes.'

'I know,' answered Charlie, sighing extremely deeply. He rested the mug on an extra-thick grease stain on his table. 'But I can't help it, you see, Joe. Life just isn't worth living any more.'

'Not-a worth living?' Joe wasn't going to stand for any of this negative nonsense. 'That's-a rubbish, Charlie, my friend. As-a my father Guiseppe used to say, "How can you be sad when the sun ees still een the sky, the birds are still-a seengeeng, and a whole world of adventure ees still waiting for you to hexplore?" You have all that and more, Charlie. Why, you even have one of Greasy Joe's world-renowned mugs of tea een front of you, ready to be-a sampled by your discerning taste-buds. I'll even throw in-a two teaspoons of sugar for you, habsolutely free.'

'No thanks, Joe,' answered Charlie, declining his friend's kind offer. 'There's no room for sweetness in my life any more—and nothing on earth now is going to change that.'

Joe departed quickly from Charlie's table; if his depression was catching, Joe didn't want any of it. He had served Charlie in this café for over fifteen years now, and he had never seen him looking so glum. Just what was wrong with his most famous customer today? Why couldn't Charlie keep all his misery in until un-Happy Hour at one?

Just as Joe returned to his normal position behind the counter, another famous person entered the smoky café: X, Charlie the Dog's boss and the strong-willed head of the ACME Peace Corporation (that was situated just round the corner). X didn't normally come to Greasy Joe's; it was much too low-class for him. But today was different. He had been summoned here by Charlie so that they could have an informal chat away from the offices of ACME.

'Ah, eet's-a Meester X,' announced Joe, saluting this highly respected man in the dangerous world of crime-fighting. 'What a pleasure eet ees-a to see you een my humble establishment. Hallow me to-a ...'

12

'Yes, yes, all right, Joe,' snapped X, abruptly interrupting in his familiar gruff voice. 'Let's have none of that fake continental charm today, please. It may fool others but it doesn't me, especially when you can't make up your mind whether you're from Italy or Spain. So if you'll just fetch me a strong cup of coffee—with at least three sugars in it! I have a feeling that any minute now I'm going to be needing as much energy as I can get.'

'Aye yi yi,' muttered Joe to himself, not in the mood to deny X's claims about his accent. 'What's-a wrong weeth everyone today? Hanyone would think that-a World War Three was going on or sometheeng.'

X, with his smart suit and posh, public-school voice, didn't quite fit in with his present surroundings. And as he waved away as much cigarette smoke as possible while advancing towards Charlie's table, most of the scruffy customers in there quickly glanced up at this distinguished tall gentleman in their midst. But they were very soon back to their grease.

Charlie was the only one in there who didn't look up. He didn't even look up as X joined him at the table; he stubbornly persisted in staring down at his untouched mug of tea, without so much as a word of greeting.

X was silent for a minute, hoping that Charlie would start the conversation. When it became apparent, however, that he wasn't going to say a thing, X gruffly began: 'So what's all this nonsense about you leaving ACME? I thought you were joking when you phoned me this morning.'

'Me? Joke?' said Charlie, making eye contact with his boss for a fraction of a second before returning to staring at his tea. 'Do I ever joke?'

'Yes, all the time!' insisted X.

'Well, not any more.' Charlie gazed silently out of the front window again, his mind obviously elsewhere. X didn't interrupt; he knew that Charlie would eventually volunteer the reason for his grey state of mind. And he was soon proved right.

After three minutes of silence, which X found irritating to say the least, Charlie began to explain. 'It's because of Agatha,' he said, still staring out of the window. 'I was glad that she finally decided to do things God's way, and for a while that lessened the shock of her death. But now...'

Charlie's voice faded away. Wisely, X didn't rush him.

Seconds later, Charlie continued: 'Agatha was the closest person I got to, X.* And now, for the rest of my life on earth, I won't have the joy of hearing her laugh, holding her hand, watching her smile, everything we used to do together. She's gone from my life—and I miss her terribly.'

'There'll be other women,' said X, who wasn't sure that it was the right thing to say.

It wasn't.

Charlie spun round to face X, and he slammed his fist on the table. X jumped. He had never seen Charlie looking so angry.

'That's not the point, X!' Charlie screamed at him. 'Not the point at all!' Then, realising that he'd been a bit too loud, he lowered his voice for the rest of his explanation. But he was still very angry.

'*Death* is the point!' he continued. 'Can't you see? It's everywhere—affects everyone! I loved Agatha, in my own way, and now she's been taken away from

---

* For full details of Agatha, please see *The Great Baked Bean Scheme*.

me. Why are the ones we love taken away from us, X? If God is fair…if Jesus is just…then why is there so much pain and suffering everywhere? I thought God was okay, but I don't know what to believe now. The world certainly isn't the nice place I thought it was. It's black, X. Black!' (Goodness. Was this the same Charlie the Dog who was normally bright and cheerful? The death of his friend must have really affected him.)

Charlie's anger was draining him. Before saying anything else, he must have some of that tea. He reached for the mug and held it to his lips. The mug was shaking as he sipped from it.

X wasn't angry at Charlie now. How could he be? He wanted to help him.

'Sorry I was impatient with you earlier,' he apologised, trying to sound less gruff than usual, which was difficult for him. 'You've been through a lot recently, I can see that. And I can see that it wouldn't be healthy for you to continue with your detective work right now. Trying to catch power-crazed super-baddies and other assorted nutters every day certainly wouldn't improve your current view of the world.'

Charlie was touched by X's unusual gentleness. After placing his mug back on the grease stain, he asked him: 'So, X, what do you suggest?'

X didn't understand this new faith in God that Charlie had; he wasn't a believer himself. But he did understand what Charlie probably needed at this time. 'What I suggest,' he answered, 'is that you forget all this talk about resigning, and take a nice long break. What do you think? Six months? A year? ACME'll still pay you during this time. It's the least we can do after all your hard work for us.'

Charlie smiled a weary sort of smile. 'Thanks, X,' he

said. 'I think I'll take you up on your offer—though I can't guarantee I'll return to ACME at the end of it.'

'You will, Charlie.' X was convinced about this. 'Detective work is in your blood. You were made for it.'

Charlie wasn't so convinced. 'Yeah, well we'll have to see about that now, won't we?'

Suddenly feeling guilty about dumping all his bad feelings on X, who'd been a sort of father figure to him over the years, Charlie reached over and gave him a gentle hug which embarrassed X no end.

'Thanks for listening, X,' said Charlie during the hug (he sounded sad as he said this). 'You're a real friend.'

'Ahem, yes, that may be true,' said X after the hug, the gruffness returning to his voice, 'but I'm also your boss. And before you go on your extended leave, you need to sign some papers back at the office to make things official.'

'Understood,' said Charlie, smiling because he knew there was a heart of gold beneath X's hard exterior. 'Let's go back to ACME now and get the signing over and done with.'

X agreed. The sooner he was out of this smoky atmosphere the better.

They both stood up and headed for the till so that they could pay for their mostly untouched drinks. The moment they reached the counter, however, 'Greasy' Joe shouted out to everyone: 'Sorry habout thees, folks, but eet's-a now-a time for un-Happy Hour.' And he changed the music on his ghetto blaster so that a tape played the ultra-gloomy Funeral March.

What was this un-Happy Hour that 'Greasy' Joe was shouting about? It was an experimental new scheme, dreamed up by the British Government, that was being tried out over a thirty-day period throughout the land. The reasoning behind it? Well, the government had noticed a disturbing amount of unhappiness and dissatisfaction among the British population in recent months, and they realised that if this wasn't controlled effectively, the nation would soon be heading for serious trouble. So, their idea was for people to hold in all their unhappiness until 1.00 pm each day, and then let it out over the following hour in whichever way they felt best (without breaking any laws, of course).

Was this emergency measure helping in any way? Only time would tell. Whatever the case, the people in Greasy Joe's Caff were certainly giving it their all.

As the dreary music played throughout the café, all of Joe's customers (except for X and Charlie) were letting their unhappiness out in some fairly unique ways.

Godfrey Biggins, a well-built trucker from Hackney, piled one Yorkie bar after another into his mouth as he snivelled and snuffled at how sad everything was. (Sometimes he snavelled and snoffled as well.) Chocolate bars calmed him down at times of great sadness like this.

Petunia Biggins, his thin, weedy wife, took all the Yorkie wrappers and wiped her tearful eyes with them because she was snivelling, snuffling and snoffling just as much as her husband. The skin round her eyes turned unusually brown as she did this, from the melted chocolate stains on the backs of the wrappers.

If you think these two were unusual, wait till you hear what Joe's other customers were getting up to.

All of them were crying as much as the two Bigginses, but in their own different ways. Some cried loudly while shooting tomato ketchup at the ceiling to express their deep frustration. Some cried quietly while shaking salt and pepper on the floor to express their own frustration. And some cried in an in-between way as they squirted vinegar at various people around them. This was because the various people were accidentally hitting *them* with ketchup and salt and pepper.

Some hid under tables as they cried because they didn't want anyone to see them. Some sat on *top* of tables as they cried because they wanted everyone to see how unhappy they were. And some hung from the light fittings on the ceiling as they cried because they liked showing off.

Many sucked their thumbs as they cried, just like insecure babies. Others sucked other people's thumbs because they wanted to be different. And some sucked their big toes, which is very difficult to do.

Basically, Greasy Joe's Caff was a very sad place to be in, and no one was sadder than 'Greasy' Joe himself. Joe was using some of this un-Happy Hour to count the day's takings so far. The takings were great—much better than average—and still Joe was crying. This just goes to show you how unhappy he was.

'Mama mia, I'm-a so unhappy, everyone,' he said to prove this, and he wiped his tears on the back of his apron because he couldn't find a tissue.

As you know, Charlie the Dog was also unhappy, but he didn't want to go over the top in expressing it. And X didn't feel comfortable when emotions of any sort were expressed, unhappy or otherwise. So they both left the café fairly quickly, after leaving two shiny pound coins on the counter.

'You can keep the change, Joe,' Charlie shouted to him as they headed out the front door—but Joe didn't hear. He was too busy yelling at a customer who'd squirted ketchup in both of his eyes.

Glad to be out of the madhouse, Charlie and X slowly strolled along to the offices of the ACME Peace Corporation. Charlie was looking forward to signing those papers so that at last he could go on a well-earned break. And X was looking forward to forgetting the smell of cigarettes.

Let's take a short break from Charlie and X right now. Before we get back to them, I need to tell you five important things:

(1) Ethel, Charlie the Dog's elderly and eccentric maid, was currently emerging from Tooting's underground station with an important paper bag in her hand. The bag contained Charlie's packed lunch (celery-and-syrup sandwiches) which she'd forgotten to give him before he left home. Ethel was wearing a gorilla costume today—without the head—and she also had on a giant cloth cap.

(2) Agent W, one of Charlie's closest friends, was handcuffed to the Fiendish Fish Finger, a human-sized batter fish finger who liked nothing better than to jump out from behind trees or buildings and scare people by shouting at them. (What a terrible super-baddy he was!) W was taking him up the steps leading to the ACME Peace Corporation building so that he could interrogate him in the cells. (The Fiendish Fish Finger had batter-covered arms—as well as legs and a face—and that was how Agent W could be hand-cuffed to him.)

(3) A fairly large (and also fairly loud) group of schoolchildren was being escorted round the ACME Peace Corporation building by Belinda Boardman, the ACME tour guide, who wasn't too long out of school

herself. (She had recently turned nineteen.) Two minutes ago she had told the fifty-or-so children (all of them nine-year-olds) to let out all their unhappiness over the next hour of the tour in accordance with British law. Belinda found it very easy to be unhappy because she'd noticed after delivering this instruction that one of the children was missing. His name was Jonathan Holden, and he had obviously gone exploring on his own.

(4) A small-ish flying saucer was hovering in the air above the ACME Peace Corporation building. The saucer was invisible at the moment, so no one in the building was aware that it was there—but they probably would be before long. You see, if the inhabitants of this flying saucer were anything like the inhabitants of other flying saucers (in comics and badly-made science fiction movies, as well as corny children's books), they were bound to get up to something unusual.

(5) Also, it would be really interesting, wouldn't it, if all these people—Charlie, X, Ethel, W, the Fiendish Fish Finger, Belinda, Jonathan, and the mysterious aliens in the saucer above—were somehow brought together and trapped in one small place? The odds against this remarkable coincidence happening are astronomical, but don't be surprised if it actually takes place. It's just the sort of crazy thing that happens in wacky books like this.

Right. Now that you know these important things, let's return to Charlie and X.

'I just don't understand it, I really don't.' This admission of ignorance was coming from X, and he was referring to all the unhappiness going on in the street around him.

Shop-owners were staring miserably out of their windows—and the greengrocer was staring miserably above his onion display so that he could cry more than anyone else. People in the street stared miserably back at the shop-owners; they were crying also, and not just because of the prices in the shops. And the traffic had come to a standstill because people found it hard to drive with their eyes full of water. Some of the drivers turned on their windscreen washers so that the cars would look as sad as they did.

'I still don't understand it,' continued X. 'I can see why people would feel down every now and then. But for people to feel *so* down, *so* unhappy. Where did all this sadness come from for the government to feel that un-Happy Hour was necessary?'

'*I* don't find it hard to understand,' put in Charlie, still in a gloomy frame of mind. 'Life on earth is terribly unfair. We're living in a far from perfect world, X, and it's just not good enough.'

Charlie was overreacting, as usual, but he did have a point. X didn't see it that way, though.

'Gaah,' he fumed, annoyed at his star detective's negative attitude. 'You won't be so pessimistic after your break. Three weeks' lying on a hot beach somewhere and you'll be back to normal, I guarantee it.'

Charlie couldn't argue with that, so he nagged at X instead. 'Anyway,' he said, 'why aren't *you* participating in un-Happy Hour? It's a criminal offence not to, you know.'

'Yes, I'm well aware of the legal implications of my non-involvement,' answered X, 'but I would rather express my sadness when I *am* sad, and not when someone tells me to. If I'm to be arrested for that, then so be it. But I don't think anyone can do much to me—

21

after all, I *am* the head of the biggest law-enforcement agency in the country.'

Charlie wanted to nag at X a bit more to get rid of more of his frustration. But before he could, Ethel had caught up with them, just as they'd reached the steps leading to the ACME Peace Corporation building. Ethel, full of apologies, was breathless from running, and sweating because that gorilla costume was hot.

'I...gasp...I...phew...I'm sorry,' she just about managed to say to Charlie as she tried to regain her breath. 'Yes, I...puff...I'm...gasp...I'm sorry... uh...that...phew...sorry, my breath, it's...'

'Yes, yes,' interrupted Charlie. 'I get the idea. You're sorry. But what for?'

Ethel answered by holding up her paper bag—and Charlie groaned. He was now even more depressed, if that was possible. He knew that the bag contained his packed lunch which he'd deliberately 'forgotten' because Ethel's packed lunches always tasted appalling.

However, he'd vowed a number of weeks ago that from then on he'd start being nice to Ethel. So he pretended to be really grateful.

'Wow. Thanks, Ethel. I'm really grateful,' he lied, putting on the best smile he could considering his current depression. The smile wasn't very convincing, but Ethel was convinced by it.

'Thanks, sir. I'd do it any time,' she responded, pleased at her boss's reaction. And there was more. 'Tell you what,' she suggested. 'To make up for the delay, I'll come up to your office and serve this personally to you on a tray.'

'Oh...goody...' Charlie was getting less convincing every second. 'Er, tell me, Ethel,' he requested, 'what exactly have you put in my sandwiches today?'

22

'Why, your favourite, sir,' she answered. 'It's crunchy celery sticks in bread, covered with generous lashings of golden syrup.'

'Fantastic...' Charlie was his least convincing ever. He wanted to get this ordeal over and done with, though, so he started his climb up the steps, with X next to him and Ethel following one step behind. They were soon inside the building.

In the foyer, by the lifts, the three of them encountered Agent W and the Fiendish Fish Finger. W was struggling because the stubborn Fish Finger refused to be pushed inside one of the lifts.

'Get in there, you fiendish piece of sea-food!' ordered W, pushing and pulling and generally doing everything he could to try and get the Fish Finger to move. But none of his efforts was working.

'Oi'm not gooing anywhere,' insisted the Fiendish Fish Finger who spoke with a thick Midlands accent. 'Oi don't wanna be interrogated. Oi wanna scare more people boi joomping out from be'ind fings.' Despicable, eh? Charlie and X weren't going to let the Fish Finger get away with this.

'Don't worry, W. We'll help you,' promised X.

'That's right,' confirmed Charlie. 'X, you make sure the lift door opens, and W and I will give that Fiendish Fish Finger a push so hard that...erm...he won't know how hard he's being pushed...or, er, something like that.'

Ethel wasn't strong enough to push a Fish Finger as tall as this one. So, because she was starving, she dipped into the paper bag while no one was looking and crunched one of Charlie's appetising sandwiches. She hoped her boss wouldn't mind too much.

'Crunch! Slurp! Guzzle!' went Ethel as she tucked into the lunch.

But Charlie and W went 'Grunt! Groan! Wheeze!' instead as they pushed the Fish Finger with all their might towards the door of the nearest lift.

Meanwhile, X was pressing the button to open the lift's door; and at the exact moment that the door opened a nine-year-old boy ran by so that he was between the struggling Fish Finger and the lift.

'So there you are, Jonathan!' shouted Belinda, the tour guide, who had just run down the stairs into the foyer. 'Stop right there! I'm going to take you back to the others!'

She ran to where he was. Bad timing! She was so intent on returning Jonathan to his schoolfriends upstairs that she didn't notice what was going on around her. The Fiendish Fish Finger was being pushed closer and closer to the lift, and if she and Jonathan didn't move out of the way pretty soon *they* would be pushed inside the lift as well.

X saw that this was the case. 'Hey! You two!' he shouted at them. 'You'd better move out of the way pretty soon otherwise you'll be pushed inside the lift as well as the Fiendish Fish Finger!' And he ran towards them to pull them out of the way.

X didn't make it in time. The moment he'd grabbed hold of Belinda and Jonathan, Charlie, W and the Fiendish Fish Finger pushed the three of them forward into the lift.

'Aw, this ain't fair!' protested the Fish Finger as he helplessly slid backwards; then they all fell to the floor of the lift after slamming into its back wall. The floor wasn't big enough for them all, so some landed on top of others. Little Jonathan was lucky. He was right at the top of the pile.

Charlie was at the bottom of the pile, but he still managed to make himself heard. 'Ethel, quick!' came his muffled voice from beneath everyone. 'Come and lift us up!'

'I'm coming!' answered Ethel who had just finished the sandwich (she thought it was scrumptious), and she ran to help her boss and his acquaintances.

It was typical of Ethel to mess things up. On the way to the lift she slipped on a puddle of grease that had dripped from the Fiendish Fish Finger. (He was a very greasy piece of sea-food.)

'Waah!' she screamed as she hurtled even faster than she had intended towards the lift. And then she went 'Oof!' as she bashed into everyone and then landed next to Jonathan on the top of the pile.

'I'm sorry, everyone. It's just that...' she started to apologise, but before she could finish the lift door closed behind her and everything went all dark. Why weren't the lights in the lift working?

Not much later the lift began moving. It didn't just rise upwards. It didn't just sink downwards. It didn't just glide sideways, or diagonally left and right. It moved in all of these directions and more at exactly the same time, which is a hard sensation to describe to someone who's never experienced it before.

It moved with incredible speed, and within ten seconds it had reached its destination. Then the lift door opened again.

Just where were they now? Were they still inside the ACME Peace Corporation building, or somewhere else entirely? Probably somewhere else entirely, knowing the freaky things that happen in Charlie the Dog adventures.

2

X's Ideal World:
Sun, Sea and…Pebbles?

'Tickets please! Can I please look at all your tickets?' This request came from an elderly British Rail inspector who was standing inside a speeding British Rail train. What does this person have to do with the story so far? Well, all our heroes (and the Fiendish Fish Finger as well) were currently on the same speeding train.

To be more precise, they were currently on the floor of a first-class compartment. As soon as the inspector had opened the door of the compartment (in perfect time with the lift door opening) their surroundings had totally changed. Their positions hadn't, though. They were still in an untidy pile on the floor.

X, after eyeing up their situation from the middle of the pile, was quick to answer the inspector.

'Er, that won't be necessary, my fine man,' he managed to say, even though Ethel's gorilla feet were pushing down on his nose and the Fiendish Fish Finger was dripping grease down his cheeks. 'I'm the head of the world-famous ACME Peace Corporation, and all of us here are currently engaged in vital work relating to the nation's security. Because of our high positions of authority, we don't need any tickets.'

X pointed to the ACME identification badge on his jacket, hoping that the inspector could see it. He could.

'Fair enough,' said the inspector, and he pulled out a pocket-sized pad from...where else?...his pocket. 'But to make things official,' he explained, 'I'll need to write you out a group complimentary ticket.'

This he did, writing on the pad in a scrawl that was worse than any doctor's. Once this was done, he ripped off the top sheet and laid it on the pile of people, between Jonathan Holden and Ethel.

'There you are, sir,' he said to X. 'Sorry to have bothered you. Enjoy the rest of your journey, and I do hope that your vital work proceeds according to plan.' He turned and slid the door shut behind him; he was now going to pick on others in the train.

'That was a close one, X,' said Charlie once the inspector had gone. 'We nearly got arrested there for travelling without any tickets.'

X smiled. 'It just goes to show you what I've always said: What's the use of having a high position of authority like mine, if you can't have fun every now and then by taking full advantage of it?'

W wasn't listening to Charlie's and X's conversation. His mind was still boggling at how a British Rail inspector could be faced with a compartment containing two men and women, a boy, a poodle, and a giant Fish Finger, all lying on top of each other in an apparently random pattern, and be so easily convinced that their uncomfortable posturing was in some way vital to the nation's security. He wondered about those who worked on trains.

'Well,' Charlie announced to everyone after finishing his conversation with X, 'now that our ticket situation's sorted out, it's time for us to get back on our feet.' Charlie was the one who commanded this because he was a natural leader, was a respected authority figure, and also because his delicate big toe was being crunched really painfully in his position at the bottom of the pile.

Ethel was the first to respond to Charlie's request. She jumped off the pile and onto one of the seats, then pulled young Jonathan onto the seat next to her.

Jonathan was naturally very confused. 'What's happening?' he said. 'I ran downstairs to try and find a loo, and now—though I don't know how—I'm on a moving train.'

Ethel patted Jonathan on the head; she thought he was cute. 'I'm afraid I don't know the answer to that, young child,' she answered him. (Actually, she wasn't answering him at all.) 'But I suspect my boss Charlie will find out what's going on. He always does.'

To make up for not being able to answer him, she offered him the second (and last) celery and syrup sandwich in her bag. Jonathan accepted this gratefully.

'Thanks,' he said. 'The crumbs from this will be perfect for my Esmerelda.'

'Esmerelda?' Ethel wondered who this Esmerelda was, but then she noticed for the first time that Jonathan was holding a small see-through plastic bag with water and a tiny goldfish inside. Esmerelda was clearly the goldfish, and Jonathan was going to spend the rest of the journey picking crumbs from the bread and sprinkling them inside the bag.

Ethel also noticed that there was a rolled-up paperback in one of Jonathan's pockets. Its cover looked really colourful. What could it be? Ethel made a mental note to ask him about it sometime. (Thank goodness she didn't ask him about it then; the best place plotwise for her to find out what the book's about is at the end of Chapter 3.)

Soon, everyone else was out of the pile as well and sitting on the remaining seats. Agent W and the Fiendish Fish Finger sat next to each other (they had to because they were handcuffed together), and Charlie and X sat opposite each other by the window. Belinda kindly stood by the entrance to allow everyone else to sit down. X was carefully holding onto the group complimentary ticket.

'Thank goodness we're out of that mess,' said Charlie, stretching all his limbs in an attempt to return them to perfect working order. 'I reckon I'm going to ache all over for ages.'

'Same here,' agreed X. 'I never want to go through that again. I'm not getting any younger, you know. My body can't take the strain.'

'So where are we all going, X?' This was Agent W talking now. 'Any idea?' (W was the ACME Peace Corporation's most handsome agent, was about the same age as Charlie the Dog—in his thirties—and was just as clever and almost as world-famous. But, of course, his skin wasn't covered with white poodle fur.)

'I'm not sure,' answered X. 'I'll take a look at the ticket.' This he did, and he gasped when he read their destination. He didn't answer for a while—just continued staring at the ticket.

'So, where *are* we going?' pushed Charlie. 'Why are you so surprised?'

'It's Eastbourne,' answered X. 'We're heading for Eastbourne on the south coast. This is exactly the place I was going to this weekend to try and find a home for my retirement.'

'Eastbourne? Great!' said Jonathan, clearly excited.

'That's the seaside, isn't it? I can go paddling in the sea, build sandcastles, hunt for shells, and loads of other things you do on a beach.'

Ethel was similarly excited, but for different, more fattening, reasons. 'The beach? Great! We can guzzle on candy floss, crunchy rock and dozens of 99s with Flakes!' Considering Ethel was such a fan of unhealthy food, it was surprising that she was so extraordinarily thin.

Charlie was excited for X. 'Now you don't have to go this weekend,' he told him. 'We might as well check out a home for you while you're here.'

And Belinda said, regretfully, 'If only the other schoolkids I was looking after were here. I just know they'd love a day out at the beach.'

The Fiendish Fish Finger was the only person who didn't say a thing, for a change. He had a dead leg from their awkward squeeze on the floor, and he was trying hard not to show that he was in pain as the grease rushed back down to his feet.

Once the pain was over, he was determined to do his best to free himself from W's handcuffs so that he could jump out from behind things again and scare more people. What a Fiendish Fish Finger he was.

The streets in Eastbourne were busy, but not too busy. The air was warm, but not too warm. And Charlie was chattering away to X, but he wasn't too chattery. This was a relief to X who had endured Charlie's frequent talkative bouts many times over the years that he had known him. X was also pleased that Charlie seemed to have forgotten about his depression now that he had a mystery to solve, though he reckoned it was probably still lingering in the back of his mind.

'What I want to know is how we ended up on that

train,' said Charlie as he and X strolled through Eastbourne's shopping area. They were followed by Ethel, Jonathan, Esmerelda the goldfish, Belinda, W and the Fiendish Fish Finger, who made quite a sight as they walked closely together. All of them were heading in the direction of the beach.

'Beats me,' admitted X. 'Have you any theories, Charlie?'

'Not yet,' he answered, and then he smiled. 'But we might as well take advantage of our surroundings while we're here. As you know, I do need a break. We'll drop in at an estate agent's for you once we've relaxed a bit on the beach.'

'Agreed,' said X, and they increased their pace. This was going to be fun.

Agent W had never been to Eastbourne before. 'There's an awful lot of old people here,' he observed, trying to ignore all the onlookers he thought were pointing at him. He didn't realise that they were really pointing at the strange-looking Fiendish Fish Finger. Some were pointing at Charlie the Dog as well because he was a nationally-renowned celebrity.

'That's right,' X quickly responded. 'Lots of people move to the south coast when they retire. And before you say anything bad about old people, W, don't forget that I'm one myself, young man!'

X gave W one of his sternest looks as he said this, a look that always made W feel terribly insecure.

'Yes, I...er...I'm sorry, X,' he apologised feebly. 'I didn't mean anything bad, you know. Why, I don't even think of you as an old person, you look that young.'

X ignored this fake compliment; he saw right through it as an attempt by W to get back into his good books. Mumbling gruffly to himself, he stepped up his pace so that they'd get to the beach even sooner.

It wasn't long before the seven of them (eight if you count Esmerelda) were facing the entrance to Eastbourne pier, and all were happy to be there because they loved days out at the beach. All, that is, except for the Fiendish Fish Finger who—as you know—was only happy when he was jumping out from behind things and scaring people. And even then it wasn't a very nice sort of happiness.

'Well, come on then,' urged X. 'What are we waiting for?' And he led them forward onto the pier where most of them had a brilliant time in the amusement arcade.

Charlie and X competed fiercely at the pinball tables. X got the highest score—at the Rolf Harris-themed table with the neon didgeridoo—but only by lifting the table up at certain points so that the ball wouldn't roll down the hole. (When you're the head of the ACME Peace Corporation you can get away with this sort of thing.)

Charlie playfully sang 'Pinball Wizard' completely out of tune to try and put him off, but it had a different effect from the one intended. Loads of old-age pensioners gathered round him to admire his attempts at tunelessness. Some sang along with him (and were equally out of tune); some clapped in time with the music, or tapped the pinball tables with their walking sticks; and one fun-loving dear breakdanced to Charlie's efforts, which is difficult to do while you're also holding on to a zimmer.

Once Charlie had finished, the appreciative OAPs chucked loads of 10p coins at him, which Charlie kindly handed to Jonathan so that he could try his luck at the 10p coin game. (This was where loads of 10p coins were piled high inside a glass case, and you tried to dislodge them by dropping another 10p inside.)

Jonathan did quite well at this (thanks to X who kicked it a number of times, much to Charlie's embarrassment—X was enjoying letting what hair he had down for once). And he spent his considerable profits on a souvenir Eastbourne stick of rock; then some souvenir Eastbourne candy floss; followed by a souvenir Eastbourne 99 with two large Flakes; and then some souvenir Eastbourne pills for his stomach ache....

Ethel, who'd wandered off on her own, was dominating the proceedings at the Bingo tables. Bingo was her very best game, and she'd won twice already, to the annoyance of her competitors at the tables. There weren't many numbers left on her present Bingo card, so it looked like she was close to completing her hat trick.

Sure enough, after another procession of 'fat ladies', strange-shaped birds and other freaks of nature that were supposed to rhyme with Bingo numbers, Ethel had crossed out the numbers she needed, and let out a blood-curdling: 'BINGOOO!!! I'VE WON, EVERYONE! BRILLIANT! I'M THE WINNER!'

While everyone else at the Bingo tables fiddled with their hearing aids (which had blown at the unusually high noise level), Ethel jumped up onto her table, then down over the other side and waved her completed Bingo card in front of the bemused Bingo presenter (in a posh black suit with tails) who wondered what planet this lady had come from.

'Okay, mister,' she snarled, thrusting out the palm that wasn't clutching her Bingo card. 'Where's my prize? Hand it over—*now!*'

34

Hiram Smooth, the Bingo presenter, calmly responded with: 'Here you are, madam. Another plastic token to show that you've won. Now that you have three of them, you can choose any prize you want from our booth over there.' With one hand he pointed to the booth; with the other he handed Ethel the relevant token; and with his lips he mouthed a silent prayer that this strange person would leave his area for good. A lady who won every game, shouted loudly when she won, and, on top of that, wore an incomplete gorilla suit and the biggest cloth cap you've ever seen, wasn't good for business. She was putting people off.

Hiram's prayer was answered. There were so many prizes at the booth that Ethel spent ages there—she was spoilt for choice. Should she claim the hilarious spinning bow tie (batteries not included); the amusing imitation nose and glasses, with bushy kangaroo-hair moustache; the rib-tickling plastic camera that squirted water at people before they could say 'Cheese'; or the chortle-inducing spectacles fitted with working windscreen wipers, ideal if you've just been squirted at by a rib-tickling camera.

Surprisingly, Ethel didn't go for any of these. Instead, she chose a frilly elastic garter with 'SUNNY EASTBOURNE' written on one side and 'HELLO SAILOR' printed on the other. Ethel didn't know any sailors so she wore the side that mentioned Eastbourne, sliding it over one of her gorilla legs. She wished her boyfriend, Norman the robot, was here; he'd love this new addition to her costume.

Now, as for Agent W: he wasn't keen on pinball, 10p-coin machines *or* Bingo. His particular favourite at amusement arcades was video games, and he was engrossed in one at the moment, sitting in a cubicle with a screen right in front of him. The game was called *Star Brek*, and it involved a starship being attacked by a gigantic lump of intergalactic porridge. Sitting down helped W feel that he was in the captain's seat (he'd always fancied himself as a starship captain), and he was currently on his twenty-third game of blasting massive great bits out of this evil floating porridge.

'There! Take that, you great big glob of goo!' W screamed at the screen as he twisted his joystick in all sorts of directions and tapped various buttons to blast powerful rays into space.

'That's it, W! You can do it!' encouraged Belinda who was outside the cubicle but could still see all through the glass panels. She found this W chap quite hunky (she'd liked him for a while), and she was doing her best to be noticed by him. To be honest, she hadn't been looking forward to this day—the thought of taking fifty-or-so energetic children on a day-long ACME tour exhausted her before she'd even done anything. But now, with W around, things had definitely taken a turn for the better.

The Fiendish Fish Finger felt differently. To him, things had definitely got worse. If W had taken him to the ACME Peace Corporation cells, which had been the original plan, then at least he would have been able to sulk in private after W had interrogated him. Now, though, he had to watch everyone enjoying themselves, and there was nothing the Fiendish Fish Finger hated more than people who were happy.

Just to spite Agent W, he tugged at the handcuffs so that the joystick W was playing with jerked violently sideways. This caused his starship to be totally swallowed up by the merciless intergalactic porridge.

'That's it, just two more hits,' W had said, 'and then I...hey! Look at what you've made me do!'

'Ooh, sorry there, mate,' apologised the Fiendish Fish Finger, sounding genuinely regretful. 'Oi fought you was soomone else.' It was the oldest excuse in the book, and W wasn't convinced by it.

'Thought I was someone else indeed,' fumed W. 'If you do that again, it's back to the ACME Peace Corporation for you.'

Now W was talking! 'Do yer mean it?' said the Fiendish Fish Finger. 'Okay, then. It's a deal.' And he obediently tugged again at the handcuffs.

The result this time was slightly different: his tug was so hard that his hand slipped right through the handcuffs (thanks to the grease that covered his entire self). The Fiendish Fish Finger couldn't believe his luck. He held up his hand. Yes, it wasn't attached to the handcuffs. He glanced at his end of the handcuffs now dangling from Agent W's wrist. Yes, they weren't attached to his hand. So what should he do now? Run. Yes, that's it. And run he did, out through the nearest exit and further up the pier. All of this happened before W and Belinda even had a chance to blink.

Once they *had* blinked, W said: 'I enjoyed that. Blinking is fun.'

Belinda agreed. (She agreed with everything W said so that he would maybe like her more.) 'Me too,' she said to prove this. 'And if you don't blink your eyes go all watery.'

Now that this small talk was over, W stood straight up and yelled 'Ow!' because he was still in the cubicle and his head had smashed into the low ceiling.

Rubbing his aching head, he stooped to leave the cubicle and said what he'd meant to say before: 'The

Fiendish Fish Finger has escaped our clutches. Let's get after him, quick!'

This they both did, shooting through the same exit that the Fiendish Fish Finger had taken. They were closely followed by Charlie the Dog and X who had also spotted the Fiendish Fish Finger's speedy escape. And Charlie was followed by Ethel who always made sure she was close to her boss.

Jonathan (with Esmerelda) chased after Ethel because he wanted to burn up some energy after all that he'd eaten, and this was the perfect opportunity. And Jonathan was followed by an amateur tuba player called Gerard Grunge, who just happened to have his tuba with him. Gerard played the theme to *Dick Barton*, an old TV show, which was the perfect tune to accompany a chase. He was always glad to be of service.

Where did the Fiendish Fish Finger run to? To the bouncy castle, that's where! He jumped straight onto it, scaring away all the children that were using it, and hid behind one of the inflatable yellow walls. If anyone passed the castle, he was going to jump out from behind the wall and scare them. Fiendish, eh? But he never had the chance to.

W and Belinda had seen where the fish finger had hidden, and they jumped onto the bouncy castle themselves. Charlie and X did likewise; then Ethel and Jonathan; and then Gerard Grunge who was still playing the *Dick Barton* theme on his tuba. The children who'd been scared away bravely jumped back on because they didn't want to miss all the excitement. Other children joined them, along with lots of adults, and it wasn't long before the bouncy castle was jampacked with bouncers of all ages. The Fiendish Fish Finger was bouncing along with everyone else, trying to dodge all the ACME bouncers so that they wouldn't catch him and slip his hand back inside those handcuffs.

'C-c-come b-back here,' ordered Charlie the Dog who almost had the Fish Finger in his grasp—but then he bounced away again.

'It-it's all r-right, Ch-Charlie,' reassured W. 'I h-have him now-wow,' he said as the Fish Finger bounced in his direction. But the Fiendish Fish Finger cleverly bounced right over him. Now he was in the path of X, who was also trying to grab hold of him. How long would all this dodging and bouncing continue?

Gerard wished this would hurry up and finish; it was hard to bounce and play tuba at the same time. The *Dick Barton* theme had never sounded stranger.

Gerard's wish was soon granted. The combined weight of everyone on the bouncy castle proved too much for the plastic it was made from. There was a pop, a phzzz, another pop, another phzzz, more pops and yet more phzzzes—until there was no air inside the bouncy castle any more and it had fallen in on itself. Before the last tower sunk down on them all, the Fiendish Fish Finger made a last desperate bounce right out of the castle.

Charlie the Dog was the second to emerge from the plastic ruins, just in time to see the Fish Finger disappearing inside the hall near the end of the pier. Gradually, Charlie's colleagues also emerged—as well as the persistent tuba player—and all of them followed him as he ran inside the hall.

Going on in the hall was a ballroom dancing competition for over eighty-year-olds, run by a smartly dressed over seventy-year-old with an exceptionally obvious wig. His name was Cedric Domeperson, and he was more than a little annoyed at these noisy intruders disrupting his competition.

Making his voice heard above the slow, old-fashioned music blaring from a prehistoric record player—while dozens of pairs of pensioners continued dancing slowly round the hall—Cedric complained: 'What do you lot think you're doing in here? Either dance or clear off—that's my final word!'

Charlie didn't feel like crossing this man—people with exceptionally obvious wigs usually had exceptionally awful tempers as well. So he ordered his colleagues to pair off and dance just like the people around them—but all the while to keep their eyes out for the Fiendish Fish Finger who was bound to be hiding somewhere in the hall.

This they did willingly (they liked a good dance): Charlie with X; Ethel with Jonathan while he still held on to Esmerelda; W with Belinda, to Belinda's considerable pleasure; and Gerard with his tuba, playing along with the music on the record player because he wanted a break from the exhausting *Dick Barton* theme. X was the most enthusiastic; he loved ballroom dancing and he was determined to win the competition. Poor Charlie was finding it hard to keep up with him.

He didn't have to for much longer. It turned out that the Fiendish Fish Finger had been hiding behind the stage curtain, and mere minutes after concealing himself there he jumped out from behind it and gave Cedric Domeperson the fright of his life.

'*Boo!*' boomed the Fiendish Fish Finger as he jumped, and Cedric Domeperson cried: 'Aaargh! It's an incredibly large fish finger, and it's going to kill me!' He was so scared that his wig shot straight up in the air then landed in Gerard's tuba. Poor Gerard couldn't play for ages because the wig had blocked his tubing.

Not noticing that his shiny bald head was now exposed for all the world to see, Cedric fled from the hall as quickly as possible, screaming: 'Gibber! It's 'orrible! I want my mummy!'

Now that he was gone, the pensioner nearest the record player took the slow, old-fashioned music off and put on a record of his own.

'Good,' he said. 'Now that boring Cedric has gone, we can dance the way we *really* want.'

There was nothing but scratching and crackling from the record to start with, but then the music started: it was a lively medley of rock 'n' roll classics, expertly put together by Jive Bunny and the Master-mixers.

The pensioners went wild to this, doing all the old rock 'n' roll dance moves. They jived and twisted and slid under each other's legs, performing moves on the dance floor that even the world's finest athletes would find hard to better. And they were thoroughly enjoying themselves.

As much as Charlie and his colleagues would have loved to have participated, they had already left the hall, chasing the Fiendish Fish Finger again who was still trying to escape from their clutches. Gerard Grunge was behind all the others in this case; he still hadn't managed to fish that pesky wig out of his tuba.

The chase led them now to the very end of the pier, and there was nowhere else for the Fiendish Fish Finger to run to because he was surrounded on all sides by Charlie, X, W, Belinda, Jonathan, Esmerelda, Ethel, Gerard and his bunged-up tuba.

'Come over here,' urged W, holding out his hand

with the handcuffs still dangling from it. 'You can't escape from us now, so you might as well give in.'

'Oh, can't oi?' said the Fiendish Fish Finger who wasn't impressed with Agent W's reasoning. 'Woi'll see about that!' And he climbed up onto the railings, ready to dive down into the sea.

'Hang on!' Charlie the Dog shouted at him before he managed to jump. 'Are you telling me you can swim? I didn't know fish fingers could swim.'

The Fiendish Fish Finger thought about this for a moment. 'You're roit,' he said when the moment was over. 'Fish fingers *can't* swim.' And he jumped back down to the floor of the pier and defeatedly held out his hand. 'It's a fair cop,' he said to W.

'Good thinking, Charlie,' W congratulated him, then he felt around inside his pocket for another pair of handcuffs. 'Here you are,' he said to the Fish Finger when he'd found them. 'Professor Boggles made these specially for me. They're greaseproof handcuffs for when I meet up with slimy nasties like you. I guess I should have used them earlier.'

As W put the cuffs on both him and the Fiendish Fish Finger, a photographer from the *Eastbourne Herald*, who just happened to be walking along the pier at that moment, requested: 'Er, could you all just turn round and smile, please? This'll make a great front page photo for next week's issue.'

Everybody immediately turned and smiled, including the Fiendish Fish Finger who liked having his picture taken. Gerard smiled while blowing into the tuba, and at the exact moment that the picture was taken the wig shot up from the horn.

Cedric Domeperson was surprised to see his wig on the front of the *Eastbourne Herald*—but he was also highly delighted. Part of him was now famous, and he went and had the picture framed so that everyone in his dance hall could see it.

At least someone was happy about the events of the day. But it wouldn't be long before Charlie and co would be wishing that they'd never ended up here in Eastbourne. Something extremely unpleasant was soon going to happen to them.

Most of the rest of the afternoon passed relatively uneventfully. They spent an hour or so listening to a brass band at the bandstand. (Gerard Grunge stayed on here because the bandleader liked his playing.) Then they watched a Punch and Judy show which young Jonathan Holden thoroughly enjoyed—it made up for his disappointment at discovering that East-bourne was a pebble beach rather than sand. (Belinda enjoyed the Punch and Judy show as well, but only because she spent the whole time glancing sideways at Agent W.) Then they trekked up to Beachy Head where they had a stunning view of the sea in front of them and the gorgeous Sussex countryside behind them. (And Belinda enjoyed the stunning view of W.)

Finally, they grabbed a load of deckchairs and lazed on the beach, watching the sea in front of them washing continuously over the Eastbourne pebbles. Charlie did nothing but look at the sea. Ethel did nothing but look at the sea. Jonathan did nothing but look at the sea. In fact, *everyone* did nothing but look at the sea. The back and forth movement of the waves, as well as the gentle splashing, was hypnotic.

Charlie felt calmed by his surroundings—exactly what he needed.

'This is the life, isn't it, X?' he said, but X didn't answer him. Not noticing his boss's silence, Charlie continued: 'But tell me one thing, X—why is it that so

.many people move to the sea when they retire? Why here? What's the attraction for them?' Again, no response from X.

Curious, Charlie turned round and gasped at what he saw. X now looked much older than he actually was, with wrinkles everywhere, thin bony arms and legs, and unbrushed tangles of snow white hair that covered the top of his head.

X wasn't the only one to have been afflicted by this mysterious rapid aging. Ethel looked older as well (if this was possible), W looked as old as Ethel, and everyone looked just as old as W, including Esmerelda who was now unusually old for a goldfish and didn't move around in her water so much because she was exceptionally weary. The Fiendish Fish Finger was so old that all his grease had dried up and great big cracks had appeared in his batter.

There was more to it than this. Stretching along the beach in both directions was a seemingly endless line of deckchairs, occupied by similarly ancient people. All of them had glazed expressions on their faces as they stared out at the sea—there didn't seem to be much going on inside their brains. And all of them looked sad—they didn't have enough strength left to be happy.

'What's happened here?' Charlie asked himself (because he reckoned no one else would be able to hear him). 'This is terrible!'

But when he looked down he discovered something even more terrible: the aging had affected him as well! The hair was thinner now on the backs of his frail poodle paws. And when he lifted them to feel his face he found that he couldn't raise them high enough; he was far too weak, too weak even to scream. He was trapped in his deckchair now, helpless to change whatever the future had in store for him. And his future wasn't going to last for much longer.

Charlie's eyes glazed over just like everyone else's on the beach, and he watched helplessly as the water advanced towards the line of deckchairs. The closer it advanced the lower the sun dropped, so that by the time the water was caressing their feet, thousands of stars looked down on them from the otherwise pitch black sky. These pin-pricks of light signalled nothing but indifference. Infinity didn't know what was going on, and the universe didn't care. It was cold—icy cold—just like the night-time breeze and the water that rose ever higher with each passing second.

It was getting harder for Charlie to think, but he still managed to conclude: 'So this is the attraction of Eastbourne. Old people come here because they know they're about to die. They have nothing to live for any more, so they surround themselves with nature, fresh air, and the sea—the immense, all-powerful, never-changing sea that calls to them. Summons them. Wants to swallow them whole. Something strangely comforting in that. Something....'

It was impossible for Charlie to think now—the aging had gone too far and his brain wasn't working too well. All that was left for him was to disappear totally into the infinite mass of the sea. What's more, he wanted it. There was nowhere else for him to go.

X wanted it as well. Maybe, subconsciously, this was the reason he'd wanted to move to Eastbourne: to die like this when he was no longer fit to work. So that he could return to the ocean (where he thought mankind had emerged from) at the end of a long, busy, tiring life. So that he could return to peace—or nothingness—at last.

The sea continued rising, and the gentle splashing

turned into deafening roaring until the violent ocean splashed above all their heads.

They were totally submerged now. The meaningless stars could be seen through the water. Charlie and his colleagues were all about to die. They were...

...back inside the lift, completely safe and only dripping slightly.

Poor Charlie the Dog was in tears. 'That was terrible,' he sobbed. 'Awful. Why did we have to go through that? What exactly is going on around here?' X was pretty upset as well.

Agent W, like everyone else in the lift, had somehow returned to his normal age. But this terrifying ordeal had made him feel that much older.

The experience had terrified him so much that he was doing what he normally did in difficult circumstances: fantasising that he was somewhere better; somewhere safer; somewhere more exciting. He was fantasising that he was captain of a starship five centuries into the future. He wore a bright red uniform; there was loads of fantastic technology at his disposal; and he had eleven crew-members under him who respected his authority and obeyed all his commands (well, most of the time).

Agent W (or should that be Captain W?) smiled in this fantasy; he felt better already. And his fantasy was so real—much more vivid than other fantasies he'd had—that not only had everyone else in the lift completely disappeared, the lift had miraculously turned into one of the starship's plush, electronic turbo-lifts. It was slowly descending.

When the lift halted and the sliding doors opened, W was faced with his messy but comfortable quarters, with a breathtaking view of deep space through the windows. Completely wiped out, he barely managed to stumble over to his desk. He collapsed into his chair, and before you could say 'Ahead warp factor ten' he had dropped off into a deep but peaceful sleep.

It was the sort of sleep that's only experienced by those who've been to death and back...and survived.

3

W's Ideal World:
Star Brek—The Next Degeneration

Space is a huge place. So huge that you could eat three million bags of salt and vinegar crisps, wash them down with six thousand gallons of sugary orange pop, then for afters munch on every piece of chocolate in existence—and *still* be able to fit inside it. Massive!

Space is even bigger than Eddie Large's tummy. This is a fact.

Captain W didn't know who Eddie Large was. This was because W lived four hundred years in the future, when, believe it or not, the once popular antics of Little and Large had been totally forgotten, as had many things from the distant past of earth's twentieth century.

W was the captain of a starship. Not a big one—it only had a crew of twelve. But it was still a very important ship.

It was called the Starship Wotasurprise, but that wasn't what made it important. It was important because it was one of a select number of starships sent out by COPPS (The Coalition of Peaceful Planetary Systems) to restore law and order in the universe. These ships didn't go after mere petty criminals. They specialised in seeking out and stopping evil baddies who were intent on taking over whole planets, solar systems, galaxies, the universe—or more!

It was all pretty dangerous stuff, and the crew of the Wotasurprise—especially Captain W—naturally had lots of exciting adventures. It's one of those adventures that I'm going to tell you about in this chapter. Exciting, eh?

Unfortunately, Captain W's current activity wasn't very exciting at all. He was snoozing at the desk in his quarters.

'Beep beep!' went the intercom on his desk.

'Zzzzzzzz,' went Captain W.

'Beep beep!' repeated the intercom.

'Zzzzzzzz,' continued Captain W.

'BEEP BEEP!' went the intercom again, louder this time. But Captain W was still going 'Zzzzzzzz.' This was like a battle to the finish. Who would give in first?

Captain W, that's who! The intercom beeped once more—as loud as it could now—and it was enough to do the trick.

'Huh? Er...what?' went W, startled at being awoken from his slumbers. 'Grief! I must have dozed off.'

He pressed a button on the intercom and spoke into it, trying to sound as calm, collected and in control (and other words beginning with 'c') as he could.

'Hello. Captain W here,' he said in a deeper voice than usual because calm, collected and 'in control' people have deeper-than-usual voices, apparently. Pretty convincing, eh? Unfortunately, the person on the other end of the intercom wasn't impressed.

'W! What are you doing in your room?' screamed a gruff female voice. 'It's time for our assignment on Random! Get yourself over to the beam-down room— *immediately!*'

'Sorry, Big Belinda,' W apologised down the inter-com. 'I didn't realise how late it was. I'll be there right away.'

Big Belinda was the Wotasurprise's security lady. She wasn't as big as Big Ben in London, but she looked like she weighed the same. She was a great big powerhouse of a woman, and had a temper that matched her size. She was definitely not to be messed with! W, even though he was the captain, was scared to death of her, but he always took her down to planets with him because she was great at scaring off baddies. Trouble was, she scared off goodies as well. (Big Belinda looked and sounded remarkably like Belinda Boardman from the ACME Peace Corporation five hundred years previously, only this Belinda weighed three times as much and was twice as tall.)

'I don't know,' W muttered to himself while he cleverly shaved with one hand, put his jacket on with the other and opened the door with his elbows. 'There's just no rest for a busy starship captain.'

Once the door was open he leapt out into the cor-ridor—which was a *big* mistake. Out there, running madly by for some reason, was Jonathan Swot, the ship's intellectual. W crashed straight into him, and his shaver flew five feet upwards, his jacket flew five feet downwards, and his elbows flew five feet side-ways which was rather painful as his arms weren't quite that long. Something else that was painful: once the shaver had flown five feet upwards, it flew back down again, landing in one of W's eyes.

'Aarrgh!' he went, which is what you say when a shaver has landed in your eye. Sensing trouble, Jonathan picked himself up from the floor and smiled feebly at the captain, sliding W's jacket back on for him to try and get in his good books. Jonathan was a bit young to be on a COPPS starship—only nine—but he was a child genius whose head was crammed with an almost unlimited amount of knowledge. All of this information was invaluable on trips down to planets, so Captain W allowed him on board the Wotasurprise, along with a full-time teacher so that he could finish off his schooling. Sometimes W regretted his decision. Jonathan *was* a genius, but he was also a bit of a coward. *And* he cracked the most terrible jokes that were always followed by an irritating laugh that sounded just like a horse neighing, only speeded up about twenty times. (And Jonathan Swot looked as remarkably like Jonathan Holden as Big Belinda looked remarkably like Belinda Boardman. *This* Jonathan, though, wasn't holding a bag with a gold-fish.)

Captain W was often annoyed with Jonathan, and today was no exception.

'Jonathan! Where are *you* off to in such a hurry?' he demanded, after Jonathan had put his jacket on.

'Erm...er...ah' said Jonathan, scratching the back of his neck and stammering nervously. 'I...er...was just heading for the beam-down room for our assignment on Random, Mr W, sir. Yes, that's what I was doing. I was.'

'Are you sure, Jonathan?' said W, suspiciously. 'You were going in totally the wrong direction.'

'Was I? Gulp. Oh, ha ha! I never did figure out where all these corridors lead to.'

He laughed like a speeded-up horse as usual, but the look on W's face showed that he thought this was no laughing matter.

'I know you better than that,' he said. 'You've chickened out again, and you were off somewhere to

52

hide. Come here, young man! You're coming with us to Random whether you want to or not!'

'Y-yes, sir! Anything you s-say...Oof!'

Jonathan went 'Oof!' because W had grabbed him by the scruff of the neck. Then he went 'Aaahh!' as he flew through the air behind W who was marching determinedly down the corridor. It wouldn't be long before they reached their destination.

Waiting for them both in the beam-down room were: Big Belinda (of course); Angus McThroatspecialist, the Scottish beam-down operator; and X the Exciting Blob Person, an earthling who had somehow been born with bright purple skin and the ability to change shape at will. Luckily his red costume changed along with him otherwise there would have been a few problems.

X's natural shape was coincidentally like a purple version of his namesake from ACME, but his personality couldn't have been more different. X, despite his title, was the most *un*exciting person in the universe. He never had anything interesting to say to anyone, he never understood jokes—especially Jonathan's— and he always had a blank sort of look on his face that showed he never quite knew what was going on. However, he was brilliant at changing shape and that was why he was on the crew of the Wotasurprise.

'About time!' Big Belinda snarled at W as they entered, then she headed for one of the de luxe plastic bathtubs at the back of the room that you had to stand in before beaming down somewhere. (Don't ask me why it was bathtubs that were used. Probably some complicated scientific reason.)

W didn't bother to respond to Belinda. It would only have provoked her even further. Instead, he remarked to X the Exciting Blob Person: 'Going to be interesting on Random, isn't it?' It was one of those things that you say when you can't think of anything else to say, and W regretted making the effort.

All he was met with was an awkward silence. X didn't reply to W; he just stared straight at him. Either he hadn't heard him, or he simply hadn't understood. Knowing X, the second alternative was the most likely one.

He didn't maintain his silence for long. Just as W was about to say something else that was equally meaningless, X finally commented: 'You've got a black eye, you know.'

'Have I?' W felt the skin round both his eyes, then clipped Jonathan round the ear. '*You* did that. It must have been the shaver hitting my eye.' Feeling suddenly weary, he urged: 'Come on. Let's beam down to Random and get this over and done with as soon as possible. I want to get back to sleep.'

W, Jonathan and X joined Big Belinda at the back of the room so that they were all standing in their own plastic bathtubs.

'Och aye the noo. Ah'm pooting ye doon noo tae Random,' announced Angus McThroatspecialist, twiddling with the dials on his beam-down console, then doing the can-can with his kilt because he was a highly eccentric beam-down operator.

'What was that?' said W, who could never understand what Angus was saying. But his question came too late. Before Angus could answer, bright orange rays came shooting out of the shower equipment attached to all the bathtubs. W, Jonathan, X and Belinda disappeared in the rays, and before they knew it they were down on the surface of the Planet Random.

'Owch!' went W, crashing painfully to the ground

because he had materialised on Random upside-down. (For some reason that always happened to him.) He rubbed his aching head a while, then looked up at his colleagues who had all materialised perfectly upright. Why did it never happen to them?

'If you've quite finished playing the fool,' snapped Big Belinda, 'it's time we got going with our assignment.'

'I know. I know,' fumed W, slowly getting to his feet while trying to avoid the hideous sight of mammoth Big Belinda in her bulging yellow track suit. 'Who's the captain here? Me or you?'

'You, unfortunately,' Belinda admitted, 'and because I'm a committed employee of COPPS I have to obey all your commands...'

'That's right,' confirmed W, pleased that Belinda had finally realised his important status.

'...so *hurry up and give us some!*' Belinda continued.

'Grrr.' Belinda was known for her bad moods, but her mood was *unusually* bad today. What was the reason? Was there something on her mind? W decided not to pursue this for the time being. He would rather get on with the task in hand.

Trying to ignore the new painful bump on his head, he surveyed their present surroundings to double-check that they'd landed in the right place. He was pleased to find that they had.

They were right in the middle of a dense forest that was almost the same as a forest on earth except for three small details:

(1) All the leaves on the trees were a striking shade of pink instead of the usual green.

(2) The grass was navy blue.

(3) Instead of squirrels happily foraging for acorns and other such edibles, there were dozens and dozens

of life-sized Ethels in gorilla costumes (without the heads) and giant cloth caps, hopping, skipping and jumping merrily around while pulling funny faces. Occasionally they scooped up handfuls of round, brown seeds from the ground and quickly gobbled them up.

As I said, though, apart from these insignificant details it was *exactly* the same as a forest on earth. (Ethels were the most common form of wildlife on Random. It was pure coincidence that Charlie the Dog's maid from earth's twentieth century looked exactly like them.)

'Great, we're here,' confirmed W, satisfied that they'd beamed down correctly. 'Now all we need to do is get to Emperor Wobbly's fortress, just six miles from here.'

Jonathan Swot put his hand up. He was about to ask a couple of his typically awkward questions.

'Yes, Jonathan,' sighed W, seeing his hand. 'What is it you want?'

'Er, um, just two things,' answered Jonathan, scratching the back of his neck even more than before because he was always scared when he was on new planets. 'Firstly, Captain, if we're...erm...so desperate to get to Emperor Wobbly in his fortress, why didn't we...er...just beam down inside his room instead of six miles away?'

'One reason,' W answered patiently, 'is that there's an invisible forcefield many miles round the fortress so that no one can beam down within a six mile radius of it.'

Jonathan nodded enthusiastically (this first reason was good enough for him), and for a number of seconds he scratched behind his knees instead of at the back of his neck so that he could have a slight change.

'The second reason,' W continued, 'is that if we beamed straight down to the Emperor this story wouldn't be as interesting. All good science fiction stories have to have exciting adventures and things set on dangerous alien landscapes.'

Jonathan didn't nod at this because it was a pretty pathetic reason. He didn't feel like arguing, though, so he went back to scratching the back of his neck and nervously asked his second question: 'Also—and I hope you don't mind me asking this, Captain, ha ha—why...er...do we have to see Emperor Wobbly anyway? What's the big deal?'

W couldn't answer this. 'To be perfectly honest with you,' he admitted, 'I haven't the foggiest. All I know is that COPPS headquarters contacted us this morning to ask that we seek him out. I presume that it's because he's some sort of nasty, evil-type baddy who's trying to take over the planet, or something even worse. You know, the usual.'

W saw that Big Belinda was about to say something like: 'Why don't you hurry up and get a move on, then?' so he saved her the bother.

'Come on, Captain W! Stop dawdling!' he shouted at himself. 'We don't have much time!'

Then he replied to himself: 'Okay! Okay! Keep your hair on! I'm doing the best I can!'

This threw Big Belinda into deep confusion so that she didn't say anything for a number of minutes. This is exactly what W had intended, and with her effectively silenced he was free to ask X the Exciting Blob Person: 'Could you become an extra, extra-tall person for us and see which direction the fortress is in? Here's a super-advanced, mega-de-luxe, state-of-the-art set of futuristic binoculars—given away free with my Corn Flakes this morning—to help you.'

X didn't sound too excited about his new task. 'Oh. Okay,' he said in a dull tone of voice, and he unenthusiastically took the cheap plastic binoculars from W.

Then, gritting his teeth, clenching his fists, tightly shutting his eyes, and using an immense amount of concentration, he cleverly shot straight up so that he was over a hundred feet tall. He was now higher than all the trees and had a clear view of his surroundings—which was perfect for his task.

The task didn't take long. He merely peered through the binoculars, turned until he saw the fortress, then shot back down again, yawning while he did so.

The Ethels were startled by X's dramatic ability, and for a moment they all panicked by loudly exclaiming: 'By gum, indeed!' and doing loads of backward somersaults. After just a few seconds of this, however, they calmed down again and returned to picking up round, brown seeds and gobbling them. Some of them even juggled with each other's dentures.

Ignoring all this strange behaviour, X informed the captain: 'It's that way' while pointing in the appropriate direction. Unfortunately, W's eye happened to be in the same direction so X accidentally poked it. W had *two* black eyes now, as well as a bump on his head from when he'd landed head-first on the ground. Poor Captain W!

W said 'Owch!' a few times—as well as a few naughty words, such as 'Underpants!' and 'Dirty socks!'—and then he urged: 'We'd better get going, then. Come on. Six miles shouldn't take us too long.' And everyone reluctantly followed.

Much to W's disappointment, their journey through the forest was pretty uneventful. So much for all the 'exciting adventures and things set on dangerous alien landscapes' that he'd hoped for. The most exciting incident during the journey was one of the Ethels running alongside them while happily waving, then ungracefully smashing into a tree because it wasn't looking where it was going.

Come to think of it, there was *one* other thing. About two miles into the walk Big Belinda started singing to herself. Now, Big Belinda often sang to herself, only this time it wasn't a lively marching song or a stirring tune about battle which is what you would have expected from her. No, it was a touching, tender love song that was at the top of the Milky Way pop charts. And she was putting an awful lot of feeling into the words, much to the surprise of W and Jonathan Swot. X the Exciting Blob Person wasn't surprised, basically because he hadn't noticed. He was in a world of his own, as usual.

After two verses of this, Belinda suddenly realised what she was singing and stopped abruptly, her face turning a deep shade of red. To cover up her embarrassment, she coughed then gruffly ordered: 'Speed up, everyone! We're moving too slowly!' and marched on ahead of them all.

W smiled. He reckoned he knew now why Big Belinda had been behaving so strangely. He decided to do some investigating once they got back to the Starship Wotasurprise.

Jonathan Swot didn't smile. He was petrified, and was scratching the back of his neck *and* behind both knees, which was quite some feat. He didn't like these assignments at all. For some reason Jonathan just couldn't cope with the constant possibility of painful death or agonising sessions of torture.

Their first possibility of pain on *this* assignment

came when they'd finally emerged from the forest. They were just a stone's throw now from the fortress, but the trouble was, its entrance was guarded by two fierce-looking soldier types, with massive great intimidating space rifles. The rifles looked as if they could inflict extreme amounts of pain, and Jonathan, hiding behind a thick pink bush with W and the others, didn't like the look of them one bit.

'Oo-er, I want my mummy,' he cried, but W calmly reassured him: 'Don't worry. I've got a plan.'

This didn't reassure Jonathan in the slightest. Captain W's plans were always very dangerous, and he definitely wasn't looking forward to seeing it in action.

The two fierce-looking soldier types, with massive great intimidating space rifles, were nattering about what had been on the vid-screen the previous evening. (One of the fierce-looking soldier types looked remarkably like Charlie the Dog, with thick, fluffy poodle fur. The other fierce-looking soldier type bore an uncanny resemblance to the Fiendish Fish Finger.)

'Did you see *Cosmic Coronation Street* last night?' said the soldier who looked like Charlie. 'Brilliant it was. They managed to fly the Rovers Pub-ship faster than the speed of light. That took a bit of quick drinking, I can tell you.'

'Nah, solar soap operas aren't moi scene,' said the soldier who looked like a fish finger. 'Oi saw the Mr Universe foinals instead. The guy representing the Milky Way galaxy were the winner.'

'Really?' The Charlie the Dog soldier sounded surprised. 'I thought Mr M-9 Galaxy was a cert to...aaaarrgh!'

'A cert ter what?'

'I said, a cert to…aaaarrgh! Look, it's a huge, angry kangatooth!'

'Oh, yeah. Oi see what yer mean. *Aaaaargh!*'

The kangatooth was the most deadly creature to be found on the Planet Random. It was almost like an earth kangaroo, except that it was ten times as big, had only one paw which it bounced continually up and down on, and had a single large tooth which protruded from beneath its upper lip. The tooth was sharp, large and deadly, and if the kangatooth managed to sink it into you, you were a gonner for sure.

'Grr!' it growled really loudly, mere metres in front of the soldiers, and they continued screaming as they nervously held up their space rifles to zap it.

They were just about to shoot when W, Belinda and Jonathan jumped out from behind the pink bush and pointed compact silver weapons (called Phearsome Phasers™) at the soldiers. Now that they were on the scene, the kangatooth no longer behaved so ferociously.

'Wh-who are you?' said the Charlie the Dog soldier.

'Never mind that now,' said Captain W, sounding cool and in command (like starship captains always do). 'Just drop those space rifles—*now!*—if you know what's good for you!'

'Y-y-yes! Anyfing yer say, mate!' said the fish finger soldier, obediently letting go of his rifle. 'Joost don't shoot those Phearsome Phasers™ or set the kangatoof on to us, okay?'

'Okay,' responded Captain W, smiling at his victory. And the kangatooth growled just one more time to show that it still meant business. When it did this its solitary tooth fell out, revealing two metal wires that were attached to it with Random Dental Service engraved on one of them.

'Oops, how embarrassing,' said the kangatooth, blushing deeply. 'Now everyone knows I've got a false tooth.' Quickly, he scooped it up from the ground, wiped the soil from it, and slipped it back inside his mouth, hoping that no one had noticed. Luckily, no one had. The soldiers were all tied up, and W and Belinda were busy doing the tying.

Once the soldiers couldn't be a threat any more, W, Belinda, Jonathan and the kangatooth (changing quickly back to X), ran through the fortress's entrance and down one of its long, winding, seemingly endless corridors.

'Well, Captain W, I must say that that was excellent thinking on your part,' Jonathan complimented him as they carried on running. 'Getting X to turn into a kangatooth was perfect. It really scared the socks off those soldiers. Erm, that's if they were wearing any, of course. I couldn't see any under their boots, but they might have been...'

W didn't listen to Jonathan droning on. He had been complimented and that was the main thing. It was fun being the captain—you were complimented on everything, even things that weren't totally your idea. (W had in fact suggested that X turn into something scary, but it was X who had chosen a kangatooth.)

Sometimes this wasn't a good thing. Poor W was about to receive a compliment that would knock him for six, and it would come from someone who *never* gave compliments.

'I agree with Jonathan,' said Big Belinda, huffing and puffing but still managing to speak as they ventured further down the corridor. 'I've been meaning to say it for ages, but I'll say it now: Captain W, I think you're brilliant!'

At this, Captain W's bones turned to ice. His every-thing else turned to ice as well. The implications of Belinda's statement were too horrific to contemplate.

When Belinda was singing that soppy love song in the forest, W had correctly deduced that Belinda was secretly in love. He'd assumed that the unfortunate target for her affections was a member of his crew, but now it was clear that the person she was in love with was him. This also explained her unusually bad tem-per today; Belinda must have been frustrated that W didn't appear to feel the same way about her.

This was awful. If he accepted her love (which he would *never* do, even if seventy deadly kangatooths were set on him) then she'd hang around him all the time, dominate him totally, and make his life a mis-ery—a fate worse than any other fate he could think of. On the other hand, if he rejected her love, she would almost certainly throw one of her infamous temper tantrums and it would take him weeks to recover.

The best thing at the moment was for him to keep quiet. There were other things he needed to worry about just now, such as trying to locate Emperor Wob-bly's quarters in this fortress.

The corridor twisted yet again. Captain W twisted with it and smacked straight into a door round the corner, with a notice on it that read: 'THIS IS WHERE EMPEROR WOBBLY IS.'

'It dooks dike we've foud our bad,' said W, rubbing his aching, bruised nose. (W now had two black eyes, the bump on his head *and* a grey, bruised nose.)

'What was that?' said X the Exciting Blob Person, who had come to a halt because there was nowhere else to run. 'I couldn't understand a word you said.'

Jonathan, who had also come to a halt (along with

Big Belinda), cleverly translated for him. 'The Captain said, "It looks like we've found our man." '

'Dat's wight, Jodathad,' confirmed the captain. 'What we deed to do dow is udlock de door.'

'Rightyho, Captain, I get the message,' said Jonathan. (The picking of electronic locks was one of his many skills.) He knelt down by the door and set to work immediately on the digital lock, which had loads of buttons and things for him to fiddle with. Trouble was, Jonathan's fiddling set off a robot guard that was massive, was heading straight for them, and was equipped with dozens of rotating tickling sticks that would tickle everyone to death if they didn't manage to stop it.

Big Belinda could hear a strange whirring sound, so she peered her head round the corner and saw the Robo-Tickler (that was its real name) advancing quickly towards them.

'Gasp,' she gasped, and she urged W and X to take a look as well. 'Gasp,' they also gasped. This was terrible.

Big Belinda was supposed to be the security lady of the Wotasurprise, so she quickly took the initiative and jumped out in front of the Robo-Tickler in a threatening kung fu-type pose. Now, what was that she'd learnt in her security classes at Earth Academy all those years ago? Ah yes: 'A good way to defeat your enemies is to give them a dose of their own medicine.' Good advice, and Belinda was going to put it into action right now.

'Come here, you fiendish metal tickler,' Belinda urged the robot, and she bounded off towards it with her arms outstretched. The machine continued advancing along the corridor, but it had to stop once it had met up with Big Belinda because she was blocking the way. Only one thing to do now: tickle her to death so that it could get past her and to the others.

Not so simple: Belinda had plans of her own. Expertly dodging all the mechanised tickling sticks, she reached forward and tickled it just above the hips. 'Take that,' she said, doing a thorough job on it.

'No—ha ha—stop it—ow—argh—owch—ha ha—you're killing me—no—tee hee,' laughed the robot in a high pitched electronic whine. (It obviously didn't enjoy being tickled.) 'Stop it—snort—I...I'm getting out of here!' And with that it rotated 180 degrees and fled from Belinda as fast as it could. This previously silver robot was now a different colour: it had been tickled pink, which was clever of Belinda (and it was also a pretty good joke).

W and X applauded her as she breathlessly ran back to them (they'd been watching all), then the three of them turned their attention to Jonathan who was still trying to beat the lock.

'I see; it looks like it's programmed using the Bingus Code,' Jonathan muttered to himself, deep in concentration. 'Could be tricky. I'll just enter a few random digits into the Yenskil Equation, cross multiply it by my highest probability factor, take away the two fat ladies, and...' Jonathan punched all this mumbo-jumbo into the buttons beneath the lock's digital display—then the display very clearly showed the words: 'YOU MAY ENTER NOW.'

'...Bingo!' continued Jonathan. 'I don't believe it! It worked!'

Jonathan leapt up in triumph, and W shook his hand. 'Well done, Jonathan,' he congratulated him. (W could talk properly again, as you can see.) 'That was pretty clever of you, sorting out the lock on the door.'

'That's right, Captain,' agreed Jonathan, smiling in

65

a way that showed he was about to tell one of his terrible, corny jokes. 'In fact, you could say I'm a-*door-able*! Ha ha! Brilliant! Get it, eh? Adorable! Titter!' And Jonathan continued to laugh uproariously at his joke, sounding just like a horse neighing, only speeded up about twenty times.

W wasn't the slightest bit amused. Neither were X and Big Belinda. (They never were at Jonathan's jokes.) Even if the Robo-Tickler had attacked them again with its tickling sticks they wouldn't have laughed—the joke was much too awful.

Deciding to move quickly on, W urged everyone to 'Shush' (especially Jonathan), stood right up close to the door, and held his Phearsome Phaser™ at the ready. Then he shouted, 'Right, here we go!', quickly kicked the door open so that he could burst inside, then found that he was pointing his Phearsome Phaser™ at...a goldfish in a bowl.

'Eh? Where's Emperor Wobbly?'

'*I* am Emperor Wobbly,' insisted the goldfish—who looked remarkably like Esmerelda, except that the real Esmerelda couldn't speak. A female goldfish playing a masculine emperor? Strange....

X, Belinda and Jonathan entered the room behind Captain W and saw what he saw: a goldfish in a goldfish bowl that was wired up to all sorts of impressive-looking computers lining the walls of the room. Every time the goldfish spoke, its bowl lit up in a kind of spooky, fluorescent green. Its words boomed from four loudspeakers—one in each corner of the room.

The goldfish continued. 'Welcome, Captain W. I've been expecting you.'

'Expecting me?' Captain W was puzzled. 'But how?'

'Easy. My computers are so clever, they can monitor broadcasts made by starships. So, Captain W, I knew that COPPS had requested that you come and track me down. They're scared, because the technology around me is now so advanced that I am able to take over the whole of the galaxy. And take it over I will—I'm going to conquer all!'

Captain W was used to dealing with power-mad maniacs like this. He found them rather boring.

'Sigh,' he went, rolling his eyes in despair as if to say: 'Not another one.' Preparing to fire his Phearsome Phaser™, he told the goldfish: 'Take over the galaxy, eh? I've met your sort before, and you haven't got a chance. One blast from my Phearsome Phaser™ and you're finished.'

'Ooh, Captain W, I'm really really scared,' said the goldfish sarcastically (which meant that it wasn't scared at all). 'You wouldn't dare fire at me. Because if you do, I'll make sure your good friend Helen gets zapped all over by my power supply.'

'Helen? What…oh my goodness!' W saw for the first time an earth woman tied up in all sorts of dangerous-looking wires in a far corner of the room. The woman was really attractive, and W recognised her instantly.

'Helen! What are you doing here?'

Helen sounded panic-stricken, a normal reaction from someone who's about to get zapped by tons of volts of lethal electricity.

'I'm panic-stricken, W,' she said, just to make things clear, and then she answered his question. 'I don't know *what* I'm doing here. One minute I'm attending to my medical duties in the Starship Yetanothersurprise. The next, I find myself beamed down here, trapped and about to die. You'd better do as Emperor Wobbly says, my love.'

'My love?' Big Belinda didn't like the sound of this.

'*My love?*' Big Belinda's cheeks were getting red with anger—redder than a ripe tomato; redder than a traffic light signalling 'stop'; redder even than Captain W's frilly boxer shorts, which were very red indeed. 'What does she mean by "My love"?' she demanded.

W was reluctant to answer her—Big Belinda wouldn't be very pleased with the truth. She'd be even more annoyed, however, if he *didn't* answer her, so he timidly admitted: 'Erm, er, Helen's an old girlfriend of mine. We were very sweet on each other during our Earth Academy days. You should know by now, Belinda, that on every adventure we have I'm guaranteed to bump into at least one old love interest of mine. The chances against all these meetings happening are staggering, yet they always occur without fail!'

'Yes, yes, I know that!' snapped Big Belinda. 'But *I* wanted to be your love interest this time, and now my hopes have been cruelly shattered. You know how frail I am!'

Big Belinda? Frail? W didn't feel like arguing with this; instead, he explained more about Helen. 'But our relationship ended years ago,' he assured her. 'We haven't seen each other since I became a captain.'

Big Belinda didn't care; there was no reasoning with her at the moment. She was in a foul rage, and she needed to do some serious venting of her frustration.

The first thing she did was kick the object nearest to her, which just happened to be one of the computers.

Crunch! went the computer, and the whole of the fortress shuddered at the force of her kick.

'I say! Stop that!' demanded the freshwater emperor, appalled at such vandalism. 'Stop that now, or Helen...' But before the goldfish could arrange for a fatal electrical charge to be diverted in Helen's direction (*and* finish its sentence), Big Belinda had kicked three more computers, punched holes in an assortment of vid-screens, and tossed six imitation penguins (with bright blue flippers on; round, trendy shades; and souvenir Rolf Harris underpants) in different directions across the room. The goldfish emperor could never figure out how these had ended up in its quarters.

The nearest thing now to Belinda's destructive hands was Emperor Wobbly's goldfish bowl. She picked it up and hurled it violently to the ground, the wires that were attached to it ripping off immediately. Surprisingly, the bowl didn't shatter, but the goldfish was helpless now that it wasn't hooked up to its computers any more.

The danger was over. They'd achieved what they'd set out to do. And it was all thanks to Big Belinda.

'Belinda! I think you're wonderful!' congratulated Captain W.

'Eh?' said Big Belinda, searching for something else to be extremely violent to.

'I mean it!' insisted W. 'The galaxy is safe once more, and we owe it all to you. Just for that, you can be my love interest for the rest of this adventure.' (W knew he was safe—the adventure was only going to last another thirty seconds.)

Belinda was overjoyed, but someone else clearly wasn't.

'You creep, W!'

'Hey?'

'I said, you're a creep!' These words came from Helen, now free thanks to X and Jonathan who thought that the captain would have wanted her untangled from all those wires. She marched over to

W. 'You told me you'd save yourself for me until the end of your captaincy. You said I was the only one for you, and promised that we'd get married and live happily together in retirement.' She lifted her fist to punch W's face. 'Why, you! You're nothing but an unfaithful old...'

The painful punch was due now, and W closed his eyes, expecting the worse. It wouldn't be long before there was another ugly bruise added to his collection.

But the punch never came. The television director responsible for this corny adventure, shouted out, 'That's all for today, folks!' after peeking at his watch and realising that if he continued a minute longer he would have to pay expensive overtime fees to the cameramen.

The cameramen gratefully turned off their cameras and started packing away. It had been a long, exhausting day.

'But, Mr Director,' protested W the actor (who clearly wasn't pleased, even though he'd been spared another bruise). 'We've almost finished. One quick punch from Helen, and then I was going to end the episode with my usual amusing "punchline" that everyone laughs at before the credits.'

W was waiting for one of his fellow actors to say, 'Oh yes, W. What punchline is that?' But none of them seemed to care. Some were heading out of the door; others were helping themselves to well-earned cups of coffee from the studio's drinks machine.

Not put off by this lack of interest, W continued: 'Yes, I was going to say to everyone, "Remember that soldier outside the fortress who looked like a giant fish finger? Well, I may be *bruised* all over, but at least I'm not *battered* like him." Brilliant, eh? Ha ha!'

No one else was laughing, basically because no one else was listening.

The director sighed and urged his lead actor, 'Come on, W. Time to get going. There's that *Star Brek* convention you're speaking at tonight, and then we want you rested so that you're ready for another hard day's shooting tomorrow.'

'Okay, Mr Director,' groaned W, and he reluctantly trudged over to his dressing room so that he could change into his twentieth-century clothes and wipe off all his bruise make-up.

Luckily, he didn't hear two of the cameramen muttering to each other about his state of mind.

'Honestly,' said one of them, 'the way he's carrying on, you'd think he really believed all this rubbish.'

'Yeah,' agreed the other. 'Sad, isn't it?'

W's convention speech that evening went well; he was always a good talker when surrounded by thousands of adoring fans of his top-rated science fiction show. It gave him lots of extra confidence; lots of enjoyment as well.

Driving home afterwards, he was stopped by the police for speeding. If he really was Captain W, he would have been able to warp on out of there and head for an unexplored planet so that he could have another exciting adventure. But he wasn't, so he had to fill in the police's legal forms and promise to pay a hefty fine.

When he got home, he discovered that his hallway light wasn't working. Things like this wouldn't happen in the twenty-fourth century he reckoned. If only he could live long enough to witness all the wonders that were in store for them then. But he couldn't. Even if he had a long life, he would barely make it to a third of the way through the *next* century.

He tiptoed upstairs as best he could in the dim light inside, and found that his wife and two sons were tucked up in their beds and fast asleep. They had been that way for a while.

W hadn't seen much of his family since he started filming the series. The hours at the studio were long.

But that was okay. It was all worth it to become a twenty-fourth-century starship captain. So wonderful. All that power. All that excitement.

'But it's not real,' he suddenly told himself, becoming very depressed indeed. 'It never was. I'm living in a fantasy world, and it'll never become a reality in my lifetime. I'm lying to myself. It's just not...'

Space around W shimmered violently at this point, as if he was in a heat-haze. A harp could be heard playing in the background.

By the time he'd finished his sentence—'...real,' he concluded—he was back inside the lift with his colleagues, who had all returned to normal.

'Phew,' went Charlie and the Fiendish Fish Finger who hadn't liked wearing those tight but impressive soldier costumes.

'Thank goodness,' said Belinda, who hadn't liked being three times her normal weight.

'Harumph! Cough!' spluttered X, who was embarrassed that he'd been forced to be a character who was so unlike his true gruff self.

'Puff! Gasp! Wheeze!' gasped Ethel, bouncing up and down in the lift because she still thought she was dozens and dozens of Ethel-creatures from the Planet Random.

'—' went Esmerelda, trying to speak (but failing miserably) because she'd liked the experience so much in Emperor Wobbly's quarters.

'Moan and groan,' mumbled Agent W, deep gloom evident in every pore of his face.

And Jonathan Holden said...Well, he didn't say anything. He'd hated the character he'd just been playing, and he was so fed up that he'd decided to read the book he'd been carrying around with him to cheer himself up. This was why he wasn't talking—he was much too engrossed.

The book was called *The Mystery of the Moaning Mansion*, and it was one of those stories where *you* decide what the main character does. It was odd: the more that Jonathan read, the more real the situations in the book became. It was as if he was actually there—feeling the rain; hearing the moaning; touching the mansion's doorbell.

You know, maybe Jonathan really was there....

4

Jonathan's Ideal World:
The Mystery of the Moaning Mansion

1

You are top detective, Sherlock Holden, and you are trapped in a lift with lots of strange characters including a greasy fish finger and the world-famous Charlie the Dog, who's almost as good a detective as you.

You start reading a colourful paperback to cheer yourself up, and as you read, the door of your lift cleverly changes into the door of a taxi. You are in that taxi, and you are heading for the infamous Very-Grave Mansion in Dartmoor where there have been reports of loud, disturbing and almost constant moaning and wailing at all hours of the day. The moaning is even worse than someone who's been given loads of maths homework to do; worse even than someone who's missed an episode of *Neighbours*.

Trouble is, your taxi driver never stops talking. He starts by talking about the weather (it is dark outside and raining); then he talks about all the famous people he's had in the back of his taxi (including the London Symphony Orchestra—it was quite a squeeze back there); then the weather again (it is still dark outside and still raining); and then he talks about his car and how well he looks after it, and how many miles to the gallon it does, and...

You have had enough. The taxi driver is boring you to tears, and you are fed up with smiling and nodding and pretending you're really interested.

You either:

(a) Scream and tell the driver to 'Shut up!' (Go to 11)
(b) Get out of the taxi immediately (after the driver has stopped it, of course), saying you're going to walk the rest of the way. (Go to 18)
(c) Rub your index finger up and down on your lips, going 'ibble-obble-ubble-obble' because you're so frustrated. (Go to bed. You need a rest.)

2

'Wooah!' you go, trying to keep your balance as you slide quickly along. The bed in this creepy bedroom stops your sliding, and you fall head-first onto it, throwing up loads of dust that was on the blankets. You also throw up soap powder and powdered oxtail soup, though what *that* was doing sprinkled on the bed you haven't the foggiest.

'Atishoo!' you sneeze because you're allergic to dust (*and* soap powder and powdered oxtail soup), and then you look up to get your bearings. Unfortunately, your bearings aren't there. You must have left them at home in the fridge.

Never mind. What you *do* see is a dimly-lit messy room, with cobwebs hanging from the ceiling, spiders hanging from the cobwebs, and 'orrible bats somehow hanging from the spiders because there isn't enough space for them in the mansion's special bat room.

There is dust (and other sorts of powder) everywhere. Dust in the corners, and dust on the door. Dust on the walls and all over the floor. Dust on the windows, and wardrobe as well. Dust on the tables, and on something that rhymes with 'well' which I can't think of at the moment.

All over the walls are paintings of moody, menacing people whom you wouldn't want to meet down a dark alley at night unless you had someone big and strong to protect you. Their eyes are so real, it's almost as if they're watching you.

And to add to the creepy atmosphere, that mysterious moaning and wailing starts yet again, and it is louder than ever before.

(Go to 16, *now*, so that you can find out what else is going to happen in this room.)

3

The room is dark and damp and not very nice. You sense there is someone in here with you, but you don't see anyone. Then you look up and can faintly see that there are scary bats just about everywhere. They are hanging upside-down from cupboards, lampshades, and anything else that bats are able to hang from.

Every type of bat is in this room. Bats with white jumpers on and pads on their legs and wings (*cricket* bats); bats that can be plucked from the very small tree in the corner of the room (*fruit* bats); and cylinder-shaped bats with lots of electricity in them (*batteries*).

You're just about to flee from this room to find somewhere safer to hide, when lots of loud moaning and wailing starts from somewhere outside the room, carries on for twenty seconds, then stops abruptly.

You look at the bats. 'Not us, guv,' one of them says to you. 'We 'ate that 'orrible sound as much as you.'

- (a) You shrug your shoulders, figuring the bats can't do you much harm, and you shut the door behind you to keep out the knight and hissing Belinda. (Go to 17)
- (b) You run back into the front hall again, to find out where the moaning and wailing is coming from. (Go to 24)
- (c) You give up and head for 22.

4

You get to England, then cycle to London. (Go to 8)

5

As you dash up those oak-panelled stairs, the moaning and wailing starts up yet again. What could it possibly be? And where's it coming from: upstairs or downstairs? You can't really tell.

Not that it matters. You *have* to go upstairs because that dangerous knight is down there in the front hall, waiting for you with his axe. (Aargh!) Also, Belinda might tell you another awful joke. (Double aargh!)

These stairs seem to last for ever. You've been running up them for ages and still haven't reached the top. What should you do? What you normally do in circumstances like these: you whip out your high powered, highly polished (and also highly expensive) magnifying glass, vital equipment for a top-class detective like you.

Still running, you examine the oak-panelled railing next to the stairs and find a message engraved in small letters in the wood. The message reads: 'PRESS DIS BUTTON 'ERE IF YER WANNA STOP', and, sure enough, there is a small red button beneath the message.

'Funny,' you think. 'I'm moving, yet the message isn't. How can this be?'

Hey! It's time for some more exciting choices!

(a) You ignore the message and carry on running, probably for ever. (Go to 26)
(b) You press the button, but I must warn you, this will lead to great danger. (Go to 6)
(c) You give up, but then you miss out on all the excitement in the rest of this chapter. (Go to 22)

6

You press the button, there is a braking sort of sound, and then it is finally obvious to all that the stairs have been like escalators, travelling down while you ran up so that you stayed in exactly the same place.

Well, you can reach the top now that the stairs are at a standstill. But the knight can also now catch you up, and he starts to chase after you up the stairs, armed with his weighty axe.

Hissing Belinda is chasing after you as well, armed

with her not-so-weighty 'Official Book of Ever-So Corny Jokes' by Anne Author. As she runs, she reads aloud an endless succession of cringe-inducing (and all-too-familiar) 'Doctor! Doctor!' jokes.

' "Doctor! Doctor! I feel like a pair of curtainsss!" "Pull yoursssself together, man!"

' "Doctor! Doctor! I like taking bathsss in sssteaming meat and vegetablesss!" "Don't get in a ssstew!"

' "Doctor! Doctor! I think I'm a ssstick of bubble gum!" "I'm going to have to chew thisss over!"

' "Doctor! Doctor! I..." '

The knight can't take this torture any more. Instead of running after you, he turns on Belinda, chasing her back down the stairs and all around the front hall.

'Help me, doctor!' cries Belinda, understandably scared. 'I'm being chasssed by a dangerousss knight with a long, sssharp axe!'

The knight, still running, replies as if he's the doctor: 'Don't worry; no *armour* will come to you. Now, *axe* me another question.'

With these two occupied, you are free to reach the top of the stairs, where:

(a) You slip on a Victorian-era banana peel, shoot through an open window and land with a thump in front of the mansion's front door. (The thump that lands with you runs off because it's scared.) The fall has made you lose your memory, but you *do* remember that you need to find out what's going on inside. (Go to 25)

(b) You slip on a soggy cake of soap and slide down the corridor into a dead creepy bedroom. (Go to 2)

(c) You slip on some greasy chips; fall through a hole upstairs; then fall through another hole *down*stairs. (Go to 12)

(d) You slip over to 22 because you've had enough and want to give up.

7

You think you can escape. The door is open, and you rush outside into the rain.

But Belinda is somehow out there waiting for you. She looks fiercer than ever, and she is pointing a threatening finger at you.

It is a chocolate finger, and she crunches it once she's used it for pointing. Then she snarls: 'Get back in there, you sssilly detective. If you think you can essscape from me, you are gravely missstaken.'

You've gulped too many times today, so you make a popping sound with your finger and mouth instead. Then you reluctantly step inside the mansion again.

Waiting for you in there is Belinda Boardman. How can she be in two places at once?

'Clever what they can do with mirrors nowadays,' she says, then she grabs you by the sleeve again and hisses: 'Ssstep thisss way. I'm going to give you a ssspecial guided tour of thisss mansssion.'

'Oo'er!' you say, not looking forward to this one bit.

(Head nervously for 14)

8

You reach London, then catch a train to Dartmoor.

(Go to 15)

9

A kanga-sledge is like a dog sledge, except that it's pulled by kangaroos. Naturally, because of all the bouncing, the ride is quite bumpy as you're pulled across the plains of Australia.

'Mush!' urges the owner of the sledge, and the kangaroos mumble things among themselves like: 'Mush? Who's he calling mush?' and, 'When they said it was a job with pull, I didn't think they meant it quite so literally.'

You don't mumble—you rumble, and it is coming from your stomach which is upset by the constant jerking movement. Luckily, it isn't long before you reach the coast of Australia. You pay the owner, wave to the kangaroos (still angrily mumbling to each other), take some tablets for your stomach, then try to find a way to get back to England.

(Go to 23)

10

'Hey, look at that,' says Belinda with a smile on her face as she points to the scary knight with the upraised axe. 'Looksss like it'sss now turned *knight*-time! Ha ha! Get it? Night-time, eh?'

You are so scared by the marching knight and his very sharp axe that you fail to laugh at hissing Belinda's joke (not that you would have laughed anyway). But then something even scarier happens that helps you forget about the knight. It's that infamous moaning and wailing which starts up throughout the mansion and carries on for a minute or two.

Belinda covers her ears to block out the sound, and so does the knight. Thinking quickly, you dive between the knight's metal legs, jump out behind him, then:

(a) Dash into a nearby room. (Go to 3)

(b) Shoot up the front hall's stairs. (Go to 5)

(c) Realise, 'Hmm. I'm bored,' and promptly give up. (Go to 22)

11

The driver is hurt by your shouting at him. He is crying, and is blowing his nose on his hankie ('Snort!' he goes) which is what you do when you're upset.

'I've never been so upset in all my life,' he sniffs while he carries on driving. 'All I wanted was a nice friendly chat with you, just to spread a bit of cheer, and look how I'm treated. Sniff! It's even worse than that time when...'

And the driver continues sniffing and droning and blowing his nose for the rest of the journey. It's even worse than when he was droning on before, and you wish now that you hadn't said anything.

You are glad when he finally pulls into the driveway of Very-Grave Mansion, and you pay him and quickly step out of the taxi. He is still sniffing and droning when you shut the door. Who does he think is listening to him?

"'Ere, where's my tip?' says a voice nearby.

'Who said that?' you wonder.

'Me,' reveals the taxi driver's smaller brother, sitting cross-legged on the roof of the taxi with a watering can. You notice him there, then realise that it stopped raining some time ago. He must have been pouring water in front of the windows to make it *look* as if it was raining.

'Come on, I want a tip—now!' he demands. 'The taxi ride wouldn't have been so atmospheric without me...so cough up the dosh!'

You realise that this person won't stop pestering you until you've done what he wants, so you hand him a fifty pence piece. He smiles, kisses the coin, then thumps the roof of the car three times. Immediately, it drives off.

Once the taxi's out of sight, lightning cracks across the sky and the rain starts again. Time for you to head for the entrance of Very-Grave Mansion so that you can get into the dry as soon as possible.

(Go to 25)

12

You fall...and fall...and fall. The fall is never-ending. Where exactly are you falling *to*? You honestly can't tell because the tunnel you are falling through is totally dark.

What you *do* know is that you're not enjoying this experience one bit. But you don't want it to stop, because stopping will almost certainly involve hitting something really hard, really quickly.

Minutes (or is it hours?) later you see a bottom to the tunnel which is round, bright and white, and is getting bigger every second. Soon the bottom is massive and you slip right through it, fall for another few feet, then realise that you are hanging upside-down in the air somewhere above Australia. You know that it's Australia because a few feet below you is Rolf Harris playing with his wobble-board in front of a camp fire. Watching him are a curious bunch: loads of bare-chested Aborigines accompanying Rolf with their hand-carved didgeridoos; a kolossal kart-load of kute koalas and kuddly kangaroos; and a gang of rough-looking workmen swigging six-packs of Tizer while twiddling with the corks dangling from their wide-brimmed hats. (Why *do* they wear those hats?) Also in the crowd is the entire cast of *Neighbours*, the most curious bunch of the lot.

(a) You look at them, say hello, then fall back through the hole. (Go to 13)
(b) You look at them, say hello, then a gust of wind blows you along so that you fall down in the midst of them. (Go to 20)
(c) You look at them, wave bye-bye, then head for 22 'cause yer wanna give up.

13

You fall…and fall…and fall—only this time you are falling *up*. The fall lasts for ages, until you fall back up into the front hall of the mansion.

Thinking quickly, you:

(a) Run to the front hall's stairs and shoot right up them. (Go to 5)
(b) Dash into a nearby room. (Go to 3)
(c) Pull the front door open so that you can run back outside. (Go to 7)

(d) Give up like the chicken you are. (What a coward! Head in disgrace over to 22)

14

Things will start hotting up soon. Not only will the central heating come on—things will begin to happen really quickly. Scary things as well. They won't be very nice.

In the minute before these things hot up, you study, with the skilled eyes of an expert detective, the impressive interior of the mansion's front hall.

There's oak panelling everywhere. Oak-panelled doors and walls, and bookshelves. Even the telly is made of oak-panelling, including the screen. It can't pick anything up, but at least it looks pretty.

There are Victorian-era paintings, Victorian-era ornaments, Victorian bits of furniture, and also a Victorian-era fax machine, which is very rare, believe me.

Everything smells old and well-preserved.

And there is creepy organ music in the background, playing on the front hall's Victorian-era CD. The music is effective.

That shiver goes back up your leg and up your spine again, and you shake, shiver and quiver because of how scared you are. You also feel cold, but as I said, things will soon be hotting up.

(a) Too scared to continue? You can give up at any time by flying over to 22.

(b) Want to carry on? Jump to 21.

15

You arrive in Dartmoor, then hire a cab to drive you to Very-Grave Mansion.

Trouble is, your taxi driver never stops talking. He starts by talking about the weather (it is dark outside and raining); then he talks about all the famous people he's had in the back of his taxi (including the London Symphony Orchestra—it was quite a squeeze back there); then the weather again (it is still dark outside and still raining); and then he talks about his car and how well he looks after it, and how many miles to the gallon it does, and...

You have had enough. The taxi driver is boring you to tears, and you are fed up with smiling and nodding and pretending you're really interested.

You either:

(a) Scream and tell the driver to 'Shut up!' (Go to 11)
(b) Get out of the taxi immediately (after the driver has stopped it, of course), saying you're going to walk the rest of the way. (Go to 18)
(c) Give up and go to 22 'cause you're getting a distinct feeling of déjà vu.

16

The moaning and wailing are very disturbing. 'I'm disturbed,' you remark, and you're disturbed even more when you notice a human-shaped lump in the bed.

'Oo-er,' you go, still stomach-down at the bottom

end of the bed, and the lump rises, a head emerges from the blankets, and the human sits up until you can see...

(There is a crash of lightning outside at this point.)

...*Belinda Boardman*, with that pale white make-up and blood-red lipstick, and the pitch black dress that looks menacing rather than pretty. Her eyes are open, but her face shows no emotion as if she's half asleep. She really looks dead creepy.

'Aargh!' you scream, and you scream 'Aargh!' even more when she pulls from under the blankets her 'Second Official Book of Ever-So Corny Jokes' by Anne Other-Author. She reads yet more corny 'Doctor! Doctor' jokes from this.

' "Doctor! Doctor! I only have fifty-nine ssse-condsss to live!" "Hold on a minute, then I'll sssee to you!"

' "Doctor! Doctor! I feel like a pack of cardsss!" "Well, ssshuffle along, then!"

' "Doctor! Doctor! I..." '

'No! I can't take any more of these jokes!' shouts a muffled voice from beneath the bed, and out rolls the knight and his axe. He jumps out, snarls at Belinda, then chases you and her out of the room.

(a) You slip on a banana peel, shoot through an open window and land with a thump in front of the mansion's front door. (The thump that lands with you runs off because it's scared.) The fall has made you lose your memory, but you *do* remember that you need to find out what's going on inside. (Go to 25)

(b) You run down the stairs, across the front hall, and into a nearby room. (Go to 3)

(c) You give up and go to 22.

(d) You stop reading altogether, and head for the

kitchen to make some cocoa. (Sounds good to me. I might just join you.)

17

But the bats *can* do you harm. As soon as you've shut the door, they jump from their cupboards, lampshades, trees, and whatever else they're hanging from, flit round the dark interior of the room for a while, then flutter in your direction until you're surrounded.

'Right,' says the leader of the army of bats (known as the *bat*talion), 'for invading our territory, young man, we're going to do something really horrible and nasty to you. It's also going to be not very nice.'

'Gulp,' you go, not liking the chief bat's threat. 'Wh-what is it that you're going to do to me?'

The chief bat wastes no time with his answer. 'We—we're going to sing the *Batman* theme to you!'

And they carry out their threat immediately. '*Batman!*' they sing together in high-pitched voices. '*Baaat-maaan!*' Trouble is, they're trying to sing in harmony, but none of them is reaching quite the right notes. The sound is horrendous, almost as bad as that moaning and wailing. Their singing is driving you *batty*.

You can't take this any more, so you:

(a) Pull open the door and run back into the front hall where Belinda still wants to tell you her corny joke. (Go to 10)

(b) Jump up and down in frustration, breaking the floorboards beneath you and falling right through them. (Go to 12)

(c) Decide to give up completely (you're a chicken at heart) and flick all the way over to 22.

18

It is raining heavily outside. You begin to wish you hadn't left the taxi, but then you remember the taxi driver's droning and realise that you did the right thing.

It is a half-mile walk to the mansion. On the way you meet a strange-looking purple person in a bright red costume. He is walking round in circles because he's not sure where he's going.

You walk round with him (getting dizzy in the process), and ask: 'What's going on here, Mr purple person with a bright red costume who walks round in circles?'

The person answers in a really boring voice (even more boring than the taxi driver): 'Oh, I'm X the Exciting Blob Person and I'm lost.'

'Lost, eh? Where do you need to get to?' (You are getting dizzier and dizzier.)

'Chapter 3. The one that's set in space.'

'Chapter 3?' you say. 'Hmm...you're only a few pages out.' Helpfully, you point down the road to where you've just come from. 'All you need to do is head back that way.'

X the Exciting Blob Person thanks you in a voice that has you bored in milliseconds, then toddles off along the road, staggering a bit because of his dizziness.

For a moment you stand there in silence, wondering if your conversation just now made any sense.

Realising it didn't, you shrug your shoulders...then, collapse because you're even more dizzy than X the Exciting Blob Person.

'Splosh!' you go, and the water beneath you thinks: ''Ere, that's not fair! *I'm* supposed to go ''Splosh!'', not 'im!'

You lie there on the ground, completely, utterly and undeniably drenched. You are also quite wet. Time to get up and head for the mansion again so that you can dry yourself out.

(Go to 25)

19

But not for much longer, because the knight comes over to you and treads on your fingers so that you lose your grip and begin to fall. What a bad knight he is!

Look on the bright side, though. If he was a good knight, then Belinda would have been able to tell you another corny joke.

- (a) You don't have much choice this time. Go straight to 12.
- (b) Didn't you hear me? 12 is your only option. Sorry.
- (c) *12! Now!* Honestly, some people....

20

Thump! is the sound that can be heard as you land next to one of the kangaroos (who's knitting himself a

.woollen track suit so that he can be known as a woolly jumper). But the kangaroo doesn't hear you, and neither can anyone else as they are concentrating too much on Rolf Harris, singing a song called 'Waltzing Matilda' really emotionally. His board wobbles violently as he gets more emotional.

You rub your aching head, then wave to one of the rough-looking workmen. The workman says, 'Gidday, mate,' and you think, 'Great! At last, someone's noticed me.' But it soon becomes clear that he was only talking to a friend of his as he passed him another can of Tizer. His friend says back, 'I'm going to put some shrimps on the barbie,' but you don't know what he's talking about because you can't see any Barbie dolls anywhere.

You like Rolf Harris and wouldn't mind listening to the rest of his song, but you know when you're not wanted. You also remember that your main task is to figure out the mystery of the moaning and wailing at Very-Grave Mansion in Dartmoor. You need to get back there as soon as possible.

(a) You make your way back to the hole, and plunge head-first straight into it. (Go to 13)

(b) You don't fancy another long fall through that hole, so you hitch a lift from the next kanga-sledge that happens to be passing. (Go to 9)

(c) You're on the other side of the world! Your task is getting increasingly impossible! You give up and go straight to 22!

21

Trying to ignore the creepy music, you glance round the room again, then gasp when you notice that the shiny knight costume previously standing near the front of the stairs, is now marching towards you with a sharp axe upraised. There must be someone in it.

You, Sherlock Holden, can be very cutting with your remarks, but that knight could be cutting in other ways. Also, Belinda has started telling you what could turn into a very corny joke.

You don't like being pursued by things with sharp axes, and you also can't stand corny jokes:

(a) So you give up, and fly over to 22.
(b) So you dash into a nearby room, leaving the knight and Belinda behind. (Go to 3)
(c) But you're so scared that you just can't move. That means you're going to have to listen to the rest of the corny joke. (Go to 10)

22

So. You want to give up.

Are you sure about this? Think about it for a while. You might be missing out on other great parts of this chapter.

(a) Come on. Don't be a chicken. Go back to where you just came from and continue.
(b) Tch. Be a coward if you wish. Flick on over to 27.

23

You board the next ship to England.
   (Go to 4)

24

As you run back into the front hall, you trip over a
Victorian-era toaster that someone has carelessly left
on the wooden floor; you fly through the air and hang
on to the Victorian-era chandelier with Victorian-era
lightbulbs from Sainsbury's; you swing from this a
bit; then you let go and fall through the fragile Victorian-era floorboards, which haven't been replaced
since Victoria stopped being queen.

Crunch! go the floorboards, and so does Belinda
because she's scoffing a chocolate finger.

   (a) You shoot right through the floorboards, not
       managing to hold on to them to stop you from
       falling. (Go to 12)
   (b) You manage to hold on to the floorboards, so
       that at least the tops of your fingers are still up
       in the mansion's front hall. (Go to 19)
   (c) You're fed up, can't stay up, and want to give
       up. (Go to 22)

25

Very-Grave Mansion is massive. Bigger than the Starship Wotasurprise. Bigger even than Eddie Large.

As you stand in front of its impressive oak-panelled door you gulp because you're scared at what you might meet inside.

You gulp again because you hear a scream when you ring the bell (normal doorbells go 'Drrrrinngg').

Then you gulp a third time when the door creaks open and a fierce-looking Belinda Boardman is revealed—with pale white make-up on her face; a pitch black dress to contrast with the make-up; and blood-red lipstick that contrasts with everything. She is quite a sight.

You gulp a fourth time because you're not sure what to say, then you gulp for the fifth and final time when she grabs a sleeve of your fashionable Sherlock Holmes-type cloak and pulls you inside. Your deerstalker hat nearly falls off in the process.

'Come ssstraight in,' she hisses, menacingly. 'We've been exsspecting you.'

'Ulp! How has she been expecting me?' you wonder. 'And who are "we"?'

The door creaks shut behind you both, and she continues hissing: 'Yesss, we have a number of interessting sssurprisssesss in ssstore for you, Sssherlock Holden....'

A shiver goes down your spine, down your left leg, then quickly out through one of your toes. It is more scared than you are.

Surprisingly, Belinda drops her fierce expression, picks it up again and puts it in her pocket, then smiles quite pleasantly while saying: 'Wotcher think of all my brilliant hissing? Creepy, eh? I spent hours on it this morning.'

What do you do now?

(a) You are still scared, in spite of Belinda's change of attitude, and you pull the door open so that you can run back outside. (Go to 7)

(b) Belinda's change of attitude calms you down a bit, so you fearlessly remain inside the mansion. (Coo. You're ever so brave. Go to 14)

26

You run for hours and hours and minutes and seconds (and lots of micro-seconds as well).

You're running out of breath, energy, and also shoes and socks because they're wearing down from all your running.

Suddenly it clicks—your brain, that is. You finally realise what's going on.

'Of course!' you say, figuring it out at last, and you kick yourself for not realising sooner. (Luckily, the kick doesn't hurt too much because your shoes and socks have worn right down.)

Then you do what you should have done ages ago: you press the button on the railing, then head for 6.

(Or you *could* give up and go to 22.)

(Important note: There is still a chance for you to go back where you came from. Come on. You can do it. Don't want to? Okay, be like that. Read on if you must. And I'll let you in on a secret—giving up like this is in fact the *only* way of getting to the end of this chapter....)

Suddenly, miraculously, you find yourself outside the mansion's large kitchen. How did you get here? All you know is that the moaning and wailing is now at its loudest. Maybe it's coming from inside here.

You open the door part-way, and witness a truly horrific sight. Chained to chairs round a table in there are Charlie the Dog, X, and W and the Fiendish Fish Finger, still handcuffed together. They are the ones doing the moaning and wailing. Why? Because Ethel, Charlie's maid, is force-feeding them a special casserole she's made from shoes, old inner tubes, and lots of other household objects that are good and useful, but not really suitable for putting in casseroles. Even Esmerelda is moaning and wailing as Ethel sprinkles dried casserole in her bowl at the end of the table. This is hideous, it really is. It's too much for you to handle.

You jump inside the kitchen, point your magnifying glass at Ethel (because you don't have a weapon on you), and demand: 'Put that serving spoon down, at once! You've no right to...'

Ethel doesn't look scared in the slightest by your magnifying glass (and why should she be?). Continuing to force-feed her poor victims, she says without looking up: 'You know, if you aren't careful, young lad, you're going to be heading for a fall.'

'Heading for a fall?' you say, puzzling over her words. 'Why do you say that?'

'Because,' answers Ethel, 'you're standing on a trap-door I've built into my kitchen floor.' And before you have a chance to run away, Ethel pushes a button in the side of the table so that the trap-door opens and you fall right through it. The tunnel underneath probably goes all the way down to Australia.

'Not again,' you say, and you go back to number...

You go back to number...

You...find yourself back in the lift because you've had enough of this *Mystery of the Moaning Mansion* adventure. It seems to go on for ever.

'Phew! Thank goodness for that,' you say. 'I'm free, at last. I thought that would never end. I'm not going to read one of those make-your-own plot books ever again.'

Everyone else (just about) is also relieved: Belinda because she isn't wearing that awful make-up any more, or being chased by the knight with the axe; and the others because they don't have to eat any more of Ethel's appalling food. The only person who isn't happy is Ethel herself; she's actually quite upset.

'Sniff! No one likes my food—no one!' Ethel weeps. 'Everyone thinks it's awful.'

Agent W feels sorry for her, so he puts his arm round her shoulder to comfort her, and insists: 'It's not that bad, Ethel! Honest!'

'You really think so?' Ethel feels better already. 'Right! As soon as we get out of this lift, I'm going to bake you a seaweed soufflé, with real seashells in it to make it more crunchy.'

'Ulp.' Agent W is beginning to wish that he hadn't been so comforting.

Charlie the Dog smiles. He's glad that other people

understand at last what he's had to put up with at home all these years.

But he doesn't smile for long. He remembers that they're trapped in this lift, and could be for ages if he doesn't act soon. Will they manage to escape before another odd occurrence happens—in Eastbourne, space, a book...or somewhere even stranger?

5

Interlude

The foyer of the ACME Peace Corporation building was alive with activity. Electricians were busy rewiring the lift so that they could get it to work again and it wouldn't be stuck. Firemen were trying to bash open the door so that they could climb up the shaft and rescue those inside the lift. And a BBC camera crew was there shooting everything for the six o'clock news. Something terrible had happened to Charlie the Dog, and the nation would want to know how he was doing.

It looked like they wouldn't know for a while. The rewiring was having no effect whatsoever, and all the bashing by the firemen made no dents in the doorway, no matter how hard they hit. It was almost as if there was an invisible forcefield there protecting it.

Derek Bowtie, the television reporter, looked deadly serious as he spoke into his microphone in front of the camera: 'Panic here at the ACME Peace Corporation building in London as firemen and electricians frantically try to...'

One of the electricians waved towards the camera at this point, shouting, 'Hello, Mum!' and smiling. Another pulled a funny face while sticking his tongue out. He'd always thought it would be clever to do that on telly.

The producer didn't see it that way. 'Oi, you two!' he said, running towards the offending electricians. 'Stop that! You're wasting valuable BBC time!'

The presenter, realising what had been going on behind his back, stopped his producer and suggested: 'Hang on. If we carry on shooting like this, with people pulling silly faces, we could get on one of those popular television specials where they show mistakes made during the shooting of films or TV shows.'

'Hey, you're right!' said the producer. This was a brilliant idea. There could be a promotion in this for him.

So, for the rest of the news report, all the electricians and firemen (and some of the ACME employees as well) pulled the stupidest faces possible, and shouted out corny jokes as well—even though it was still un-Happy Hour. (It was all in a good cause.)

This meant that they weren't working on the lift, but that was okay. For all the good they were doing, they might as well not have been there at all.

Meanwhile, in the lift:

'I wonder if anyone's trying to rescue us,' said Jonathan, imagining his face in the papers the next day. This was exciting.

No one else shared in his excitement, though. The last few minutes (or was it hours?) had been a bit too much.

Agent W was upset that being the captain of a starship wasn't as exciting as he thought it would be.

X was still upset by his disturbing experiences in Eastbourne.

The Fiendish Fish Finger was upset that his wrist was held tightly in Agent W's handcuffs.

Belinda was upset that W didn't appear to feel as strongly for her as she did for him.

Ethel was upset that no one liked her cooking.

Esmerelda was fed up with being in this tiny plastic bag—not enough room to do anything in there.

Charlie was still hugely upset about the death of his friend, Agatha Smethwick.

And all of them (except Jonathan, who didn't understand the seriousness of their situation) were extremely, incredibly (and very) upset that they were trapped in this freaky ACME lift, maybe for ever. Who knew what might happen next?

Funnily enough, even though Charlie had been expressing doubts about God back in Joe's Caff, he was now fervently praying to him. He still didn't understand the meaning of Agatha's death, but he did know that when it comes to the crunch and you're in a helpless situation like this, God is really the only person you can turn to.

'Help!' he started praying (which is always a good thing to pray). 'We're stuck, and we can't do anything! We can't get out through the panel in the ceiling.' (Charlie had already tried. It mysteriously refused to budge.) 'We can't get out through any panel in the floor.' (Charlie had tried to find one, with no success.) 'Nothing happens when we press the emergency button.' (He was telling the truth.) 'So, basically, we're in a fix. Only you can help us now.'

Ethel shouted out a loud 'Amen!' because she thought it was the right thing to say. She'd also had her eyes scrunched up and her palms pressed tightly together. (Charlie had had his eyes open the whole time as he pleaded heavenwards.)

No one else had joined Charlie and Ethel in their praying, but, with the exception of X, they really didn't mind too much—even the Fiendish Fish Finger, who didn't care where his freedom came from, as long as it came soon.

X was the only one who was annoyed by the praying. He waited a few seconds after Ethel's 'Amen!', then coughed and grunted (which is what he did when he was annoyed) and gruffly barked: 'Well, Charlie, fat lot of good *that* did us! Your God, if he's even listening, hasn't helped us at all. But then I could have told you that before you started. Praying is a waste of time.'

Charlie had to protest. 'But…' he started to say, but then it occurred to him that maybe X had a point. Bad things happened in this world—that fact was undeniable. One of those bad things was Agatha dying. And now there were all these strange experiences in this lift. Why did bad things happen, when God was supposed to be real? Maybe prayer *didn't* achieve anything. But if that was the case, who could you turn to at times like this?

Charlie searched desperately for the words to finish his sentence, but was rudely interrupted by a booming, deep voice that was so loud it made the walls of the lift vibrate.

'Ahem, er, hello,' started the voice. (Like Charlie, it was also obviously struggling for words.) 'Sorry about the delay, but our computer's struggling to take in all that we've seen so far.'

Charlie was quick with his response. 'Who are you?' he shouted, looking heavenwards again because he wasn't sure where else to look. 'You mentioned "we". Does that mean there's more than one of you? And why have you kept us in this lift to force all these horrible experiences on us?'

The voice sighed really loudly, then responded with: 'My goodness. Why is it that whenever we capture specimens from an alien culture to study all their innermost secrets, they want to know who we are and our reasons for doing things to them?'

Charlie's voice now rose in anger. 'You've captured us here against our wills! You're exposing our personal desires in front of each other! The least you can do, if you have *any* decency, is to tell us your names and what your intentions are! Why, this really...'

'Hold on,' interrupted the voice, and its volume lowered as if it was talking to a colleague away from its microphone. 'What's that? The computer's ready again? Great stuff!' The volume increased, as the voice addressed those in the lift again. 'We can continue now, everyone. No more questions. It's time to visit the ideal habitat of the one who calls herself... *Belinda Boardman!*'

'Now, just one moment!' protested Charlie. 'You can't do this to us! It's just not...'

But he was too late. The mysterious voice had already put into operation the next stage of its scheme.

In the second before Charlie the Dog disappeared, an interesting thought occurred to him: 'Maybe God doesn't intend to rescue us yet. Perhaps he has other plans.'

And in the second before the Fiendish Fish Finger disappeared, he had managed to slip his hand out through the handcuffs again without Agent W knowing. So much for Professor Boggles' greaseproof cuffs. The fish finger was determined never to be captured by W ever again.

Everyone else disappeared as well, except for Belinda Boardman. The lift door opened in front of her, and she heard the sound of an on-board motor, and the trickling and splashing of water.

What could be waiting for her outside?

GREETINGS (SORT OF) FROM THE POODLE TRIBE!

6

Belinda's Ideal World:
Problems with the Poodle Tribe

Belinda walked bravely through the doorway, and just about everything around her turned to wood. That was because just about everything around her was now a wooden house boat which smelt of wood, wood polish, wood, damp wood, more wood polish, and wood yet again. But that wasn't all that changed. Instead of the posh outfit she had on when guiding people round the offices of ACME, she now wore a bright, flowery, short-sleeved shirt, a dried-grass skirt, deep pink flip-flops, as well as similarly-coloured flowers in her hair.

So, where was she? She walked to the side of the boat, leaned over, and looked down. She saw that the boat was slowly moving along a river, and a low, distant hum was coming from a motor somewhere that was little more than idling. The water was perfectly clear.

'Hmm,' she thought. 'I don't know any clear rivers in England. Maybe I'm in a foreign country.'

This suspicion was confirmed when she looked across. On both sides of the river, as far as she could see, was a pretty dense jungle. No, it wasn't attractive and unintelligent. It was *pretty dense*, which meant that there were trees everywhere, vines in between the trees, and lots of other exotic foliage fitting in the best it could between everything else. Belinda had never seen so much plant life squashed together like this before.

Then, when she looked up she saw that there wasn't a cloud anywhere in the sky, which was therefore blue all over and not the miserable sort of grey that Belinda was used to. The sun, beating down (and up, and across, and in all other directions as well), was totally unobscured. In fact, now she came to think of it, it was unbelievably *hot, baking and sweltering out here. Phew!*

'My, it's hot,' said Belinda. She was glad that she wasn't wearing that much.

'Too right, love,' agreed someone nearby. Someone nearby? Who could that be?

His name was Humphrey W and he was sipping cool Vimto from a cocktail glass with an umbrella in it (even though it wasn't raining). He was reading a *Beano Summer Special* while relaxing in a striped red deckchair; he had trendy mirror sunglasses on, with lenses shaped like five-pointed stars; and he also had a knotted flowery handkerchief laid on top of his head, with the initials HW embroidered in one corner. (He had actually stolen this from Hotel Weymouth, but don't tell anyone, will you?) Apart from the hankie and glasses, all he had on was a pair of baggy brown shorts held up by braces that partially covered his pale and not-very-hairy chest, and a pair of Marks & Spencer underpants on underneath. There was also a pair of handcuffs dangling from one of his wrists. Goodness knows why *they* were there.

'Oh, my! It's W!' exclaimed Belinda. This was too

good to be true. 'You're here. *We're* here. I mean— *together!* It's...'

'Together? Of course we're together, my love!' W was puzzled by Belinda's confusion. He pushed his glasses up to his forehead so that Belinda could see his puzzled eyes, but he didn't mind too much when they fell back into place because the glare from the sun was really quite strong. 'We booked this holiday months ago, after that incident in the ACME Peace Corporation lift when we realised how much we loved each other. "A private cruise deep in the jungles of Africa," said the brochure. "What a perfect romantic location for our honeymoon," you said. So here we are now, newly-wed and very happy because we're the most perfect couple ever in the whole of the history of all mankind.'

This really *was* too good to be true, reckoned Belinda. But there was no denying that it was actually happening to her. The best thing to do was just enjoy it.

'Ah, yes—ha ha—of course,' she laughed, flapping her hands in an embarrassed sort of way. 'Silly me. Of course we're on our honeymoon. All this heat must have made me forget.'

'Ho ho,' W laughed back, even though what Belinda had said wasn't the slightest bit funny. (He was obviously in love.) 'Here—you obviously need a rest. Grab a deckchair and sit next to me.'

'Good idea—hee hee,' giggled Belinda, and she snatched a folded-up deckchair from the floor next to W and folded it out into the shape of a comfortable chair...erm, sort of. Actually, it was a bit of a mess.

'Oh dear, that doesn't look right,' Belinda correctly observed, and she promptly folded the deckchair into another shape which looked even less like a chair.

'Hmm, that's worse,' she continued observing, realising there was no way she could sit on *that*. She hadn't realised deckchairs could be bent into such strange shapes.

'One more go,' she announced, determined to get it right this time, and she wheezed, grunted, puffed and groaned as she manipulated the wooden frames backwards, forwards, sideways, diagonally, then backwards again, until she was left with...a complete and utter fiasco that may have started life as something resembling a deckchair but certainly didn't end up like that. Her arms were caught near the top, her legs were stuck at the bottom, and she couldn't move to save her life.

Good job W was there to help her. But he didn't. He was far too comfortable to move. Instead, he rang a hand bell by his deckchair and an elderly deckchair attendant immediately emerged from the same doorway Belinda had appeared from. (He was included in the price of the cruise, and was on loan from Hyde Park in London.)

'Can I 'elp you, sir?' he enquired, tipping his hat politely.

'Yes please, my man,' said W. 'Events seem to have rather caught up with my wife. Could you help her out of her fix?'

'Certainly, sir,' answered the deckchair attendant, and he obligingly loosed Belinda from the jumble of wood and fabric, cleverly twisted it into its proper shape as quick as a flash, then stood in front of W, tipping his hat again as if to hint that he himself would quite like a tip.

Realising that this was the case, W flicked through his *Beano Summer Special* and ripped out a page.

'Here,' he said, handing it to the deckchair attendant. 'Have the Little Plum story for your efforts.' (W was ever so generous.)

'Little Plum, sir? Brilliant!' said the deckchair attendant, gratefully receiving the story from Humphrey W. 'Plum um my favourite character. I am goin' to like um this. Chuckle!'

As the deckchair attendant disappeared back through the doorway, W wondered out loud: 'Why is he chuckling? Did he make um joke or something?'

Belinda—reclining comfortably now on the properly made-up deckchair—giggled when W said this. 'Speaking of jokes,' she said between chortles and titters, 'since we're on the deck of a boat, we should call what we're sitting on *deck*-deckchairs! Snort!'

For the briefest of moments, W wondered whether he'd done the right thing by marrying this strange lady. But then he fell in love with her all over again, basically because he loved the way she guffawed like a pig being tickled or merrily chewing on the *Beano Summer Special*.

The rest of the day was relatively uneventful. W lazed on his deckchair, Belinda lazed on her deck-deckchair, the deckchair attendant read the Little Plum page over and over again in the comfort of the boat's wooden cabin, and all was as it should be on a lazy, sweltering, bright summer day.

Only once did Belinda break the silence before it turned night. It occurred to her that since they were in a foreign land, there might be some interesting wildlife underwater.

'W, you gorgeous hunk,' said Belinda.

'That's me,' admitted W, mumbling because he was only half-awake. 'What is it you want, O love of my life?'

'We're in Africa, right?'

'That's correct, sugar plum!'

'Any interesting creatures in the water?'

W stood up from the deckchair—for the first time that day—and peered over the side of the boat to examine the river more closely.

'Well, delightful one,' he answered, 'there are a few old crocks in there at the moment.'

'Crocodiles? Really?' This was exciting. Belinda jumped up from *her* deckchair and joined W in peering over the side of the boat.

What she saw was not quite what she expected: an endless procession of ancient automobiles, driven by equally ancient Englishmen and women. The cars were half-floating in the water as they travelled in the opposite direction to the boat.

'I say,' one of the drivers (a retired colonel type) called out to W. 'Any idea where we are? We need to get to the old crocks race in Brighton, and I reckon we're a teensy bit lost.'

W pointed them in the right direction, then returned to the comfort of his deckchair. He really was a lazy old thing.

Belinda was equally lazy, and as she returned to the comfort of *her* deckchair, night fell really quickly (in the space of two-and-a-half seconds—apparently, it does that sort of thing in the jungles of Africa). Thoroughly enjoying the sight of the stars all around, she mumbled happily: 'This is so relaxing, it would be nice to fall asleep to some music.'

'Easily taken care of, sweet honey pie,' responded W, and he rang his bell *two* times. This was the cue for the cruise's special musicians to enter. Would they be a string section? A barbershop quartet? A modern, mellow jazz group? Something soothing, relaxing and nice?

None of these things. Sorry. The musicians (if that's the right word for them) who emerged from the cabin were greasy, hairy and smelly, and the dark leather jackets they were wearing looked as if they hadn't been cleaned since they came off the animals they originally belonged to. It was the famous thrash heavy metal trio who went by the name of Leatherhead.

'All right!' screamed the tough-looking lead singer and bassist, while the others set up their equipment behind him. 'I suppose you two morons want some music!' (Being rude was part of his stage act—although he managed to be rude in real life as well.)

'Erm, yes please, Mr singer, sir,' answered Humphrey W.

'Hmph. Okay, I suppose so.' The singer turned to his colleagues. 'All set up now, you scumbags?'

'Yer, dat's right,' said the lead guitarist, and the drummer nodded his head, throwing loads of his long hair forward so that it totally covered his face.

'Well, about time, that's all I can say,' grunted the lead singer, and he faced W and Belinda again. 'Right, you lucky dimtwits. Here we go with our latest hit single, "Bash Your 'Ead Between Two Bricks".'

'Oh goody,' said W. 'I like this one. It's nice.'

The band started up really loudly. The guitarists plucked away at their strings like there was no tomorrow, no next week and no next century either. The drummer thumped away like there was going to be no *anything*, and in a totally different rhythm to anyone else in the band. And the lead singer sang like there was gravel in his throat, enough to cover an average suburban driveway.

These are the words he sang:

I don't want to dance all night.
Boogie on down, or get in a fight.

113

Don't want to listen to great guitar licks.
I just wanna bash my 'ead between two bricks!

Don't want to eat much rhubarb fool.
Taste it hot, or sample it cool.
Don't want to call yer between five and six.
I just wanna bash my 'ead between two bricks!

And so on for six more verses. I would include the chorus, but it's just not worth it. All it consisted of was different words like 'Yow!' and 'Owch!' as the lead singer carried out the advice of the song (something the reader should *not* do as it can be quite painful—and you could break valuable bricks as well).

Leatherhead wasted no time once the song was over. This trio of scruffy yobbos went straight into their next song: 'Bash Your 'Ead Between *Three* Bricks', which was intended to be their follow-up single. Then they played every hit single they'd had in their long and varied career. (Their set lasted fifteen minutes.)

W and Belinda weren't awake by the end of the set. The music had had the effect they desired, even though it was far from soothing, and they were dozing even before the end of the first song.

Just before she'd dropped off, Belinda had thought while gazing up at the multitude of stars, gazing across at her beloved W, then gazing up at the multitude of stars again because W couldn't be seen very well in the darkness: 'This is perfect—just perfect. Who'd have thought all those months ago when we got trapped in that lift, that we'd end up married like this? I never want this honeymoon to finish—ever. I...'

And then she was asleep, with a great big smile on

her face because she was more content now than she'd ever been.

Bliss. Wonderful bliss. But how long would it last?

It was 3:55 in the morning. 3:55, and W was asleep, Belinda was asleep, the deckchair attendant was asleep in his cabin, and Leatherhead were asleep on the floor next to their instruments because they were totally wiped out.

Everyone was asleep, it seemed. Everyone, that is, except for a handful of very strange people in the jungle. Any moment now, they were going to dive into the river, but they were obligingly waiting for me to describe them before they did so. Thanks, chaps!

Their names were Charlie-woof, X-woof, Ethel-woof, Jonathan-woof and Esmerelda-woof (or Es-woof for short). Why did they all have 'woof' at the ends of their names? Because they were members of the poodle tribe, which is so obscure that only two-and-a-half people know about it. Charlie-woof was the chief of the tribe, basically because he was the only real poodle among them.

'I like being the chief of the poodle tribe,' he would often say to himself.

'*I* like being the chief of the poodle tribe as well,' Ethel-woof would say to *her*self, but Charlie would tell her off because you can't have two chiefs of a tribe.

When you were a member of the poodle tribe you wore imitation white poodle fur all over: on your legs, your arms, your body, and on your head as well, except for your eyes, ears, nose and mouth, because if you couldn't see, hear, breathe or talk, you wouldn't be a very effective member of the poodle tribe. Sometimes Charlie-woof wished that *Ethel-woof*'s mouth was covered, but you can't have everything, even when you're the chief of the poodle tribe.

There were only two exceptions to this dress code: Charlie-woof who had fur of his own, so didn't need to bother with this imitation stuff; and Esmerelda-woof whose costume would have been soaked if she'd worn one, and that wouldn't do. To make up for this, the bag that Jonathan-woof kept her in was covered all over in the finest quality imitation poodle fur that you could find anywhere, even Purpleland (next to Greenland) whose main industry was the manufacture of imitation poodle fur. Trouble was, Es-woof couldn't see out of the bag, and no one could see inside to wave hello to her. This was the sort of thing you had to put up with when you were a dedicated member of the poodle tribe.

One more thing about the poodle tribe: they loved to tie people to trees, then dance round them, waving plastic bones in the air and slapping their mouths while screaming so that they sounded like police sirens. No one ever got hurt, but it was still a scary experience for those who were tied to the trees.

The poodle tribe hadn't done this for ages, basically because so few people passed through this very remote part of the jungle. Therefore, when they heard the raucous singing of Leatherhead, five of the tribe ran to the riverbank immediately. They were desperate to run round someone else again. It had been ages.

Right, I've finished my description of the poodle tribe. You can jump in the river now, chaps!

'Yeah, and about time too,' grumbled Charlie-woof. 'I thought you'd *never* stop talking.'

Charlie-woof turned to his colleagues in the tribe, switched on his jungle torch (powered by special jungle batteries), and pointed at the water as if to urge them to jump inside.

'I see *you're* not going to jump in again,' observed Ethel-woof. 'You never swim in this river. I reckon you're a scaredy-cat!'

Charlie-woof didn't appreciate this criticism. 'Me, scared? Of course not, Ethel-woof! How dare you even suggest such a thing!' He was clearly offended. 'It's just that...it's just...well, *I'm* the chief of the tribe, so *I* need to stay here and supervise.'

Young Jonathan-woof was sniggering to himself. He covered his mouth up to try and hide this, but he wasn't doing very well.

'What's so funny, Jonathan-woof?' said Charlie-woof, still upset that someone had challenged his swimming abilities. 'I don't see that there's anything to laugh about.'

Still sniggering, Jonathan-woof answered: 'I've just realised—tee hee—Ethel-woof should have called you a scaredy-*dog* instead.'

Charlie remained stoney-faced, and the others agreed with him: there *wasn't* anything to laugh about. Ethel-woof and X-woof dived quickly into the river so that they wouldn't have to pretend to laugh at Jonathan-woof's attempt at a joke. And Charlie-woof kicked Jonathan-woof in behind them, for obvious reasons. This meant that Esmerelda-woof was in the river as well, because Jonathan-woof was holding on to her bag.

X-woof and Ethel-woof did their job speedily and quietly. They swam up to the boat, pulled themselves inside, kidnapped the sleeping bodies of Humphrey W and Belinda Boardman, then skilfully swam back to shore with them. Jonathan-woof, meanwhile, dithered and gibbered in the water, not getting anywhere

117

because he was a scaredy-*human*. He was frightened because of all the dangerous crocodiles, or alligators, or rare African piranhas (normally found in South America) that might be in there.

He needn't have been so worried. All the crocodiles, alligators and piranhas had fled from the vicinity as soon as they'd heard Ethel-woof's voice. They could bite through most things, but not through Ethel-woof's leftovers which she often threw into the river in large quantities because no one would eat her food. When they'd tried to bite through it, it had tasted so appalling that they'd been sick for weeks. They didn't want any more reminders of Ethel-woof's cooking and how chronically ill they'd been.

'Come on, Jonathan, that was pathetic!' scolded X-woof on the way back to shore with W over his shoulder. 'You're nothing but a useless lazybones.'

Jonathan sniggered again, forgetting his fear. He pulled an imitation bone out of his pocket beneath the water, and held it up for X-woof to see. 'Actually,' he said, in between sniggers, 'I'm a *plastic*-bones! Get it?'

X-woof groaned, and so did Ethel-woof and Charlie-woof. Esmerelda-woof merely sighed. Why did she have to be carried around by Jonathan-woof? If she heard any more fish jokes (such as: 'Hey, this bag I'm holding seems a little *fishy*! Chortle!') she was going to scream. Trouble was, no one would be able to hear her through the thick insulation of the imitation fur-covered bag.

Once the still-sleeping bodies were safely on shore, and the giggling Jonathan-woof had been fished out of the water by X-woof and Ethel-woof, Charlie-woof gave the command for them to advance through the jungle so that they could rejoin the rest of the tribe and have fun with their captives.

Jonathan-woof was a bit put out by their non-reaction (as well as sopping wet). 'Why doesn't anyone laugh at my jokes?' he called out. 'They're not that bad, are they?'

It was obvious what everyone's answer would have been if they'd replied. But they didn't bother. Instead—with the exception of Es-woof—they speeded up their pace so that they could get further away from Jonathan-woof and he wouldn't be able to pester them any more.

When Humphrey W and Belinda awoke, they didn't at first realise what was going on.

'Hmm. How are you doing, my beloved?' asked W, after yawning and partially opening his eyes.

'Huh? Whassat?' mumbled Belinda, after yawning and not opening her eyes in the slightest. The familiarity of W's voice had finally woken her up.

W's eyes were watery, so he lifted one hand to rub them. Or at least he tried to. His arm wouldn't move. Why exactly was that?

He opened his eyes a bit more partially.

Then partially even more.

Finally, they were fully open and not partially in the slightest. Through the water—which was starting to dry—he saw that his arm was tied by a rope to his body. He tilted his head and saw that his other arm was tied in a similar fashion.

He wriggled a bit then realised that his whole body was tied to something, probably a pole of some sort from the feel of it against his back. His suspicions were confirmed when he looked across at Belinda and saw that she too was tied to a tall, thin, wooden pole.

Belinda's eyes opened at that moment (about time) and she looked across at W looking across at her. They both gulped—'Gulp!' 'Gulp!'—when they realised they were probably being held captive by someone.

Then they both looked round, and saw for the first time hundreds, and dozens, and dozens, and hundreds of very strange people holding smooth white plastic bones, in a clearing in the jungle known as the poodle village.

Why were they strange? Well, the holding of the bones for a start. Secondly, they were all wearing imitation poodle fur costumes. This meant that W and Belinda were surrounded by—yes, you've guessed it—the little-known poodle tribe in its entirety.

Its entirety, of course, included Charlie-woof, the chief, who was standing directly in front of W and Belinda. Actually, this wasn't entirely accurate; he couldn't be directly in front of *both* of them, could he? He was more sort of in front of the centre of an imaginary line that joined the two poles. Glad I could clear that up.

Anyway, Charlie-woof—directly in front of whatever it was that he was directly in front of—cackled maniacally at W and Belinda while waving his bone about a bit, then announced to them: 'Welcome to the village of the poodle tribe. We're going to dance around you a bit now. Erm, I hope you don't mind.'

Ethel-woof was disgusted. 'Don't be so polite!' she rebuked the chief. 'When you're the chief of a tribe you're supposed to be loud and intimidating.'

Charlie-woof thought about this for a moment, then concluded: 'Yeah, Ethel-woof, you're right.' And to make up for his previous politeness, he screamed at W and Belinda: *'We're going to dance and dance until you can't take it any more! We're going to scream like police sirens until you go completely deaf! And we're going to starve you until you're so hungry that you'll eat any-*

thing... even Ethel-woof's food! Erm, if this is all right with you, that is.'

Before Ethel-woof had a chance to complain—about his slur on her cooking, as well as him reverting to politeness again—Charlie-woof smashed his bone down on his bonce three times, which was the signal for the tribe to start doing their stuff.

Which they did. Most of the hundreds, and dozens, and dozens, and hundreds of them gathered round the two poles and danced like they'd never danced before, waved their bones in the air like they'd never waved their bones in the air before, and slapped their mouths while screaming so that they sounded like police sirens like they'd never slapped their mouths while screaming so that they sounded like police sirens before. It was really quite something.

The accompaniment to all this dancing came from a rhythm section to the far right of W. X-woof clicked and clacked with a pair of small metal spoons; Y-woof (his brother) rattled a shiny tin of dry jungle peas; and 'Woof-Woof' Wakeman, the keyboard virtuoso of the tribe, was playing the jungle bongos really quickly. Actually, it was an electronic keyboard with the sound of bongos programmed into it; he insisted that this was better than the real thing.

W and Belinda felt sick. It was awful being trapped like this. Who knew what terrible things might happen to them?

Jonathan-woof felt sick as well. He was sulking in front of his straw hut (made from thousands of bright pink drinking straws). Why did no one laugh at his jokes?

To cheer himself up, he made another joke up on the spot.

'Knock knock,' he started.

'Who's there?' he continued.

'Bongos.'

'Bongos who?'

'Bongos this way, and the other goes that way! Cackle!' And he laughed even more maniacally than Charlie-woof had. (You could tell that he'd made this up.)

No one else laughed maniacally. They didn't even titter politely—that was because they had their minds on other things. This was useless. Jonathan-woof went back to sulking and sighing really deeply. Es-woof sighed deeply as well, but for different reasons.

'I don't know,' Jonathan-woof mumbled. 'I'm not appreciated round here. It's just not...hang on a moment. Who's that over there?'

The 'who' that Jonathan-woof was referring to was a human-sized batter fish finger with arms and legs and a grease-covered face. It was hiding by a nearby straw hut (made out of *blue* drinking straws) where it thought that no one could see it. But Jonathan-woof could, and he was going to warn the chief. This fish finger person might be up to no good.

Jonathan-woof darted up to the chief, and tugged the paw of his that wasn't waving a plastic bone in the air.

'Here, chiefy!' urged Jonathan-woof while tugging. 'There's something really important that I need to tell you.'

But Charlie-woof, dancing with the rest of his tribe round those poles, waved away this annoying little pest.

Jonathan-woof was persistent. 'B-b-but...' he continued, but Charlie-woof continued to wave him away.

Meanwhile, Belinda and Humphrey W were having

a worried conversation. They were both really panicked.

'Darling W,' sobbed Belinda, 'you're an ACME agent. If you really, really love me, slip free from your ropes somehow and get us both out of here.'

W did love Belinda, so he strained, and grunted, and flexed his muscles as far as they would flex, but he didn't manage to loosen the ropes in the slightest.

'Sorry, O wondrous Belinda,' apologised W, shrugging his shoulders as far as they would shrug. 'Despite all my super ACME strength, I can't seem to break free.'

This wasn't good enough for Belinda. 'Come on, W, my sweetness,' she urged. 'You can do better than that for me, I know it.'

'Okay, I'll have another bash,' agreed W, and he grunted and strained, and stunted and grained, and flexed his muscles even further than they could flex, which was pretty difficult, believe me. But there was still no snapping or creaking sound from the ropes. It looked like he and Belinda were well and truly stuck.

But not for much longer. The Fiendish Fish Finger made himself known to the poodle tribe at that point. He jumped out in front of the blue hut and shouted out, in the loudest voice he could manage: 'Boo!'

His dramatic entrance had the effect he desired. Half of the poodle tribe fainted, and the other half went 'Gasp!' and 'Gulp!' and 'Golly!' while quaking in their imitation poodle fur costumes. Belinda went 'Gasp!' as well, but W's reaction was altogether different.

'It's you!' he screamed. 'I've been after you since you escaped from me in that lift. I'm not going to let you out of my clutches ever again!' And with all of the fierce determination that can be found in every agent

123

that works for the ACME Peace Corporation, he flexed his muscles like he'd never flexed his muscles before until—creak, groan, snap—he was free! Would he help his wife escape? The thought hadn't even crossed his mind. All he was concentrating on at the moment was catching that nasty fish finger and trapping him in the other end of his handcuffs again.

'Ooh, my goodness, it's 'im,' said the Fiendish Fish Finger, seeing the furious W heading straight for him, and he dived back into the depths of the jungle.

Belinda was furious. W hadn't managed to rescue her, but he'd made every effort to pursue this Fiendish Fish Finger. Men—they were all the same: only bothered about their own interests. And she thought she'd found such a good husband in W. What a disappointment.

Charlie-woof was flabbergasted by the effect this fish finger character had had on his tribe. In fact, his flabber had never been so gasted before.

'Why didn't anyone warn me this was going to happen?' he raged, because he didn't like things to be out of his control.

'B-but,' continued Jonathan-woof, still tugging at the chief's paw, but chief Charlie-woof cut him off. He knew what Jonathan-woof was going to say, and he didn't want to give him the satisfaction of being right for once.

This is what he cut him off with: 'Right, everyone,' he commanded those around him who hadn't fainted, 'let's get after that fish finger thingy. We'll teach him to interrupt us when we're having some fun.'

They obeyed Charlie-woof quickly, following him into the jungle. They were quite glad at this new bit of excitement in their otherwise dull existence.

Jonathan-woof didn't rush off (and therefore neither did Esmerelda-woof). He was sulking again.

'No one appreciates me. No one,' he grumbled, thinking it, but also saying it out loud without realising.

'*I* could appreciate you,' said a female voice to his right.

'Huh? Who said that?' said Jonathan-woof, looking up and around. When he saw Belinda still tied to the pole, he realised that she was the one who'd spoken to him.

'It was me,' confirmed Belinda, 'and as I said, I *could* appreciate you, but only if you'll release me from this pole.'

Jonathan-woof had to think about this for a moment. He really shouldn't, not until the poodle tribe had finished dancing round her. But he was desperate for appreciation. What should he do?

He stood up, that's the first thing he did. Then he said: 'Oh well. I really could do with the appreciation. I'll just have to avoid chief Charlie-woof for the next few days.' Then he strolled over to this Englishwoman and calmly untied the ropes that held her to the pole.

'There we go,' he said when he'd finished, and he took a step back so that Belinda was free to move. He felt pretty pleased with himself, and he couldn't wait to receive some of her appreciation.

The appreciation didn't come. Letting the ropes fall to the ground, she rudely pushed Jonathan-woof to one side, hissing: 'Get out of the way, kiddo!' then ran the best she could in her high heels towards the others in the jungle.

Jonathan-woof was more miserable than ever now. 'She took advantage of me. I'm ever so sad.' He looked down at his fur-covered bag and softly said, 'Well, at least you still like me, don't you, Es-woof?' And he opened up the bag to peer inside at his one and only friend.

His 'one and only friend' squirted water up into both of his eyes.

'Byeurgh!' went Jonathan-woof, and he wiped his eyes with one hand and quickly closed the bag with the other. Then he sat cross-legged on the ground and rested his chin on his fists. This was the unhappiest he'd ever been—even more than that time his stand-up comedy routine lost at the poodle tribe's recent talent show, scoring fewer points than Ethel-woof's ten-minute cookery demonstration.

Poor Jonathan-woof. It really wasn't easy being the least-liked member of the remote and little-known poodle tribe.

It wasn't easy chasing the Fiendish Fish Finger through the thick, hot African jungle either. There were thick, hot African trees in the way all the time. And if it wasn't trees, there were thick, hot snakes crawling along the ground, with other assorted jungle creepy-crawlies. Something else in this jungle was thick and hot: a British Rail ticket collector who'd recently eaten a curry. But he wasn't in the way. He kindly stepped behind a tree when all the chasers raced past him.

'Phew, oi'm puffed,' gasped the Fiendish Fish Finger as he jumped over jungle-type things, ducked under jungle-type things, and dodged in between jungle-type things as well.

'I'm going to get that fish finger, if it's the last thing I ever do,' puffed the determined Humphrey W, dashing past jungle gibbons, jungle parrots, jungle lions, and a jungle penguin as well because this was a very strange part of the jungle.

And the remainder of the chasers—roughly half of the poodle tribe—dashed in and out and under and over each other in their mad scramble to be the first to catch up with the Fiendish Fish Finger. The one who wanted most to catch up with him first was Charlie-woof, but he wasn't doing very well. He was lagging at least six thick, hot trees behind everyone else, and showed no signs of improving his speed. This really wasn't a good show from the chief of a remote and little-known poodle tribe.

Eventually the Fiendish Fish Finger ran out of jungle to run through and ended up by the bank of the river. Coincidentally, it was the same part of the river that W's and Belinda's boat was on. Leatherhead, still on the boat, were currently giving a free concert, entertaining the crocodiles, alligators and piranhas, who had gathered round in the water because they liked loud music. The deckchair attendant didn't, though, and he was miserably sitting on one of his deckchairs, his arms stubbornly folded, his face screwed up grimly, and lots of fluffy cotton wool sticking out of both of his ears so that Leatherhead would maybe get the hint and stop playing. Unfortunately, they didn't.

With nowhere else to go, the Fish Finger turned to face all his pursuers. As they charged towards him, he threatened: 'If yow lot come any closer, oi'll shout "Boo!" again, all roit?'

That stopped them! W halted just centimetres in front of the Fish Finger, and the poodle tribe halted as well, even Charlie-woof who was way behind the others.

What should they do now? They were stuck. It

seemed that it was up to the Fiendish Fish Finger to make the next move.

Not necessarily. A voice on the river behind the fish finger shouted: 'Your time's up, fish finger! I have something here that you're not going to like!'

'Huh? Who wuz that?' And the fish finger turned round to see Jonathan-woof floating up behind him on the river. He was sitting cross-legged on a log, and the log was being pushed along by Esmerelda-woof, splashing energetically behind it.

The thing that Jonathan-woof reckoned this Fiendish Fish Finger wasn't going to like was a big greasy frying pan that belonged to Ethel-woof. And it turned out he was right. The Fiendish Fish Finger hated frying pans, for obvious reasons (they reminded him of death), and he shook, shivered and shook a bit more because the last thing he wanted was to be fried until he died—crisp and crunchy and ready to eat.

'Gasp!' he gasped.

'Shudder!' he shuddered.

And when he gasped again, Humphrey W clicked the other end of his handcuffs round his wrist which meant that...he was trapped again! Hooray! Yippee! At last!

But not for much longer. Belinda emerged from the jungle just then, storming, and stomping, and stupendously stoney-faced.

'Humphrey W, there you are!' she screamed. She clearly wasn't pleased. 'How dare you leave me all tied up like that! Now I know where your priorities lie! You're nothing but a no-good...'

I won't tell you what Belinda said after 'no-good' because it wasn't very nice. What the Fiendish Fish Finger did wasn't very nice either. In the commotion, he managed to quietly slip his hand out through those handcuffs again and tiptoe back inside the jungle. When W realised what had happened he screamed at Belinda who was still screaming at him. The noise was unbearable—louder even than Leatherhead!

Charlie-woof couldn't stand all this racket—neither could the rest of the poodle tribe. Wanting an excuse to leave quickly—and not even questioning how Belinda had managed to escape—he calmly strolled over to the riverbank and said to Jonathan-woof: 'Thanks for doing your best to save us from that horrible fish finger.'

Jonathan-woof, still on the log, blushed in a happy sort of way and modestly shrugged his shoulders. 'Well, it was nothing really, chiefy. If the truth be known, it was Esmerelda-woof here who showed me this short cut along the river to where I reckoned the fish finger was heading.'

'Yes, but you were the one who was brave enough to confront him,' insisted the chief. He held out his paw so that he could lift him off the log and back onto dry land. 'Come with me. We're going to celebrate your bravery back at the village.'

'Oh really?' said Jonathan-woof as he allowed the chief to pull him up. 'Wow. At last I'm going to be properly appreciated by the fellow members of my tribe.'

'Yes,' continued Charlie-woof, holding Jonathan-woof's hand so tightly that there was no way he could escape, 'in your honour we're going to tie you to one of those poles and dance right round you all night.'

Jonathan-woof sighed. What a disappointment. He should have known that this had been too good to be true. To try and cover up his sadness, he joked: 'Being tied to that pole is going to be hard for me to bear. In fact, you could say it's a *pole*-ar *bear*! Brilliant, eh?' Actually, it was pathetic. And no one laughed.

Esmerelda-woof didn't swim back to the village. She was thoroughly enjoying Leatherhead's heavy metal music, and she banged her head repeatedly on the bank of the river, which is the sort of silly thing you do when you listen to music like Leatherhead's.

If only W and Belinda were as happy as Es-woof. They were still shouting loudly, at exactly the same time as each other so that one didn't know what the other was shouting.

That booming deep voice—the one they'd all heard in the lift in Chapter 5—wasn't happy either.

'These earthlings,' it mumbled to itself, not realising that it could be heard. 'Aren't they ever satisfied? We're trying to find an ideal habitat for them, but something always seems to go wrong. This Belinda Boardman—we thought she would be happy with her one and only true love, but obviously this wasn't good enough. What are we to do with them?'

The voice stopped booming for a moment—stopped saying things out loud that it knew already so that the reader could learn a bit more about what was going on (and very kind of it, too). Instead, the voice listened to an important suggestion that its colleague was making.

'Hmm, yes, you're right,' it said to this suggestion. 'The goldfish seems to be the only one enjoying itself at the moment. So let's transfer everyone to the fish's ideal world, and see what happens there. Maybe we'll have more luck.'

And with a wave of this alien's hand (or rather, the pressing of a button in its spaceship) it was so.

7

Esmerelda's Ideal World:
What a Lotta Water

'This is brilliant—fantastic! This is absolutely ace!'

Leatherhead weren't around any more, and neither was there any music (not that Leatherhead and music had anything to do with each other). There were no alligators or piranhas either. Esmerelda the goldfish was in heaven.

Well, not really. She was at the centre of a seemingly infinite amount of water, free to swim wherever she wished. After being trapped in that tiny plastic bag for so long, this certainly seemed like heaven.

She swam forwards.

'Luxury!'

She swam backwards.

'Brilliant!'

She swam sideways in both directions. (Esmerelda was a very clever goldfish.)

'Terrific!'

She swam up, then down, and then forwards and backwards, and sideways in both directions again.

'Splendiferoso!'

Then she began to feel that something was missing. What could it be? It certainly wasn't water that was missing.

She thought for a moment.

She thought for another moment.

Then after a third moment of thinking, she realised that her owner Jonathan wasn't nearby, nor any of the people she'd begun to count as her friends since the start of this business in the lift.

She stopped swimming and tried to sense what was going on in the water around her. She could feel frantic vibrations coming from somewhere above her head.

'Hmm, wonder what's causing that,' thought Esmerelda, and she swam up and up and up, until…

'Oh dear, it's all my colleagues, and they're desperately gasping for air.'

Esmerelda's observation was correct. Charlie, X, W, Jonathan and Ethel—all of them in their normal everyday clothes and none of them wearing imitation poodle fur outfits—were twisting their limbs in certain directions, gyrating their bodies in other directions, and shaking their heads in the remainder of directions that were available to them, because they were desperate for air to breathe (as if all this panicked movement would help them find air). No doubt the Fiendish Fish Finger was elsewhere in the water, twisting in similar directions himself.

When this struggling group saw that Esmerelda was in their vicinity, they looked at her with pleading eyes and held out pleading arms. They wanted a quick end to their suffocating.

Esmerelda was desperately unhappy about what she saw. All this water was heaven to her, but while her colleagues were suffering in it, it could never be anything more than a form of hell. She would rather be back in her small bag so that they'd be all right. She would rather…

She was back...somehow.

So was everyone else—in the lift, that is—except for the Fiendish Fish Finger who was still roaming free somewhere.

They were miserable, dripping wet, and doubted that things could get any worse.

Jonathan might have cracked a joke about them being big drips, but he wasn't in the mood.

8

Ethel's Ideal World:
Room at the Top

Ethel, Charlie the Dog's maid, was wet. (So was everyone else.)

Ethel, Charlie the Dog's maid, was gloomy. (So was everyone else.)

And Ethel, Charlie the Dog's maid, was talking. (No one else felt like talking.)

This is what she was saying: 'I'm fed up. I've had enough. I want to go home—now!—and forget that any of today ever happened.'

Without thinking, she pressed the 'DOORS OPEN' button in the lift. This was a silly thing to do, as the lift was obviously under the control of mighty alien powers, so she shouldn't expect the doors to open as easily as that.

However, for a silly thing to do, it was surprisingly effective. The lift doors opened out into Charlie the Dog's hallway, as if all in the lift were coming in from his front garden pathway.

'I don't believe it,' said Ethel. 'We're home—back at Charlie's house!' And she leapt into the hallway before the lift doors had a chance to close again.

The others didn't believe it either, but they weren't going to miss their one and only opportunity so far to be free from this lift for ever. They followed Ethel into the hallway, and once they'd all done so, the lift doors quickly closed behind them and cleverly turned into Charlie the Dog's front door.

Freedom! No more horrors in obscure English seaside towns. No more disappointing adventures on dangerous alien landscapes. No more being trapped in a hurriedly-written make-your-own-plot book. No more sweltering heat in Africa, or gasping for air in infinite water. At last they'd been returned to normality. Well, almost—but at least Charlie the Dog's home would do for the time being.

All of them were excited enough to talk again, and they filled the cramped confines of the hallway with their noise.

Ethel kept repeating, 'It's great to be free again—it's wonderful to be free.'

Jonathan said to Esmerelda in her bag, 'Fantastic! I've always wanted to visit a famous person's house.'

W, X and Belinda kept saying, 'Rhubarb! Custard! That yumptious yoghurt which you can buy in milk-type cartons!' because they wanted to contribute to the general noisiness of the occasion and couldn't think of anything better to say.

But Charlie butted in after not too long: '*Belt up*, the lot of you! You're giving me a headache!'

Everyone obeyed, except for X who hadn't heard the command.

'...which you can buy in milk-type cartons!' he concluded really loudly, and then he realised that everyone was looking at him. 'Ahem...er...cough,' he went, trying to act as if he was the most senior person in the room (which he was) but failing miserably. 'Just...er...just giving you all the chance to be quiet first so that you wouldn't be embarrassed.' What a feeble explanation.

'Well, come on then, everyone,' urged Ethel. 'What are we waiting for? Let's all head inside and enjoy our freedom.'

Ethel barged on through to the rest of the house, and shouted out to her robotic boyfriend, 'Norman, we're back! How're you doing, chum?'

There was no answer, so Ethel shouted again, 'Norman, where are you? We want to see you and say hello!'

Still no answer. Ethel shrugged her shoulders. 'He must have gone shopping,' she said while her shoulders were still shrugged. Then, when she unshrugged them, she offered: 'Sit yourselves down in the living room, and I'll make us all a nice hot cup of tea.'

Tea sounded brilliant, except to Charlie who knew what Ethel's tea tasted like. But he needn't have worried.

'What's wrong here?' she shouted from the kitchen to everyone patiently waiting in the living room. 'The stupid kettle's not boiling!'

'Maybe the fuse has gone in the plug,' Charlie shouted back to her. 'Why don't you boil some water in a pan instead?'

'Good idea, sir,' Ethel answered, and she promptly did this. A shame that this didn't work either.

The next thing shouted from the kitchen was: 'The cooker's not coming on! This is useless!'

'Let's have some cold drinks, then,' suggested Charlie, who was rather relieved about the tea.

'Okay, sir. Right you are.'

It wasn't long before Ethel entered the living room bearing a tray containing ice-cold cans of different types: Vimto, Tizer, Diet Vimto, Diet Tizer, Caffeine-free Diet Vimto, Caffeine-free Diet Tizer, and one of those hilarious, rib-tickling cans from which three or four compressed giant worm-thingies shoot out when you lift off the top.

'Anyone want to try an exciting new drink?' Ethel said as she offered the tray round to everyone.

'Me, please,' volunteered X, sticking his hand in the air like an eager schoolboy. He would try anything once.

'Okay.' Ethel gladly handed him the dodgy can.

The unsuspecting X lifted the top off the can. Then...

Fwoosh! went the worm-thingies as they shot up out of the can, bounced off the ceiling, and skilfully landed in the goldfish bowl across the room, one after the other.

'Waah!' screamed X, who stupidly hadn't expected this to happen.

And then everyone laughed at this highly amusing (and highly unoriginal) practical joke. Everyone, that is, except for Charlie the Dog who had seen this joke many times before and was totally fed up with it. He almost snapped at Ethel about her boring practical jokes, but then thought better of it. He'd only be opening a can of worms.

Once everyone was settled down with their drinks and sitting comfortably on the sofa or bean bags on the floor, Ethel suggested: 'Okay, everyone. How about a video to keep us entertained?'

Charlie almost told Ethel off again because he knew what was coming (and it was exceptionally boring—even more boring than the can with the worms). But then he thought, 'No, I'll let Ethel enjoy herself. She deserves it after all she's been through today.'

Jonathan was the first to shout 'Yes!' because he

liked watching videos, especially comedies. Ethel took this to be a 'Yes!' from all of them, and she snatched from her bookshelf the most treasured video in her collection: four whole hours of Ian McCaskill's BBC weather reports recorded over the last few years. (Ethel was Ian McCaskill's biggest fan.)

'You lot are going to love this,' she assured her colleagues as she slotted the video in the recorder and switched on the telly. She sat back and waited for Ian's calming tones to begin.

She waited a bit longer.

She waited even longer than that.

And then she said, 'Hmm, something's gone wrong here,' and she crawled back over to the video machine.

She pressed the play button. Nothing happened.

She pressed the rewind button. Nothing happened.

She pressed the fast forward button. Nothing happened again.

Then she pressed the eject button and something really horrible happened. The video itself came out, but not all of the tape that belonged inside it came with it. *Scrunch! Scrunch!* were two of the sounds that greeted her ears after pressing 'eject'. Another two sounds were *Scrrsh! Snap!* Correctly suspecting the worst, Ethel pulled the video from the recorder and saw to her horror that the tape had snapped and some was stuck inside the machine. The further she pulled the video away from the recorder, the more tape unwound from inside it.

Ethel had gone pale as if she felt sick (which, coincidentally, she did). 'Oh dear,' she said, quietly and gravely. 'It took me years to put that tape together. Now it's ruined...for ever.' She was too shocked to cry. She just stood there, horror-struck.

Charlie quickly crawled to her side of the room,

knelt down beside her and put a paw round her shoulders.

'Cheer up, Ethel,' he comforted her. 'I'll take it to the lab at ACME. I'm sure the gang there'll be able to fix it for you.'

'Thanks, sir,' said Ethel, her voice trembling softly. 'Can I take everyone upstairs and show them my Smartie-lid collection instead?'

Charlie looked round at everyone and tried, in his expression, to convey that 'this is going to be really boring, you lot, but please go along with her—she needs cheering up'.

They got the message, and it wasn't long before all were trailing up the stairs, with Ethel leading the way to her bedroom. They were privileged; not many people got to see this most private of places.

Ethel had perked up already; she was enjoying all this attention.

'I started my collection of lids off the tops of Smartie tubes ten years ago,' she explained as she thumped loudly up the stairs in her gorilla costume. Her oversized cloth cap flapped wildly with each movement she made. 'Each Smartie lid has a letter on it, and my aim eventually is to use them to spell out the entire works of Enid Blyton. So far all I've managed to do is all the Mallory Towers series, plus a couple of the Secret Sevens. But I'll be finished one of these days, you wait and see.'

Charlie, behind Ethel on the stairs, turned and gave everyone another one of his expressions, this time communicating: 'Yes, I know she's mad, but humour her, all right?' Charlie waved his finger round one ear to show what he meant. Everyone was glad to humour her; they actually found Ethel quite likable.

Once she'd reached the top of the stairs, Ethel led

everyone down the upstairs corridor until all were gathered by an ancient wooden door that was covered from top to bottom (and from left to right as well) in stickers of many types. Some were big stickers; some were small stickers. Some were round; others were square-shaped or triangular. Some were colourful; some were only black printed on white (or white on pitch black). Some looked old and faded; others looked like they'd only been stuck on this morning after breakfast. But despite all these differences, they had one thing in common: all bore the strange warning 'BEWARE THE TEETH!' Why this particular warning? Because as soon as Ethel opened the door, hundreds of sharp, deadly, dangerous false teeth were activated on Ethel's floor. They were cleverly set to come on whenever the door opened.

'Clatter! Clatter! Clatter!' clattered some of them.

'Click! Click! Click!' clicked others.

And ' ' went the remainder of them because their batteries had run down. Never mind. There were still enough false gnashers snapping up and down to scare even the hardest of criminals. They scared Charlie the Dog as well.

'Sorry about the teeth, everyone,' Ethel apologised above the din. 'Try and tiptoe between them all so that you can come inside.'

This everyone did, extremely slowly and carefully, and remarkably none of them got bitten even once by the dentures. As they entered, they gasped at the state of Ethel's room—except for Charlie who'd been in here many times before, and Ethel who couldn't understand why everyone was gasping.

This is what they saw:

The walls, ceiling and floor (under the dentures) were covered with posters, magazine articles and signed colour photographs of Ian McCaskill, along with imitation BBC weather maps. Hanging from the ceiling with ancient string were loads of pots and pans—covered in varying thicknesses of rust—that Ethel had used over the decades and had kept as mementoes of her work as a maid. Some still had decades-old fried egg stains on them, and others had flakes of prehistoric dried casserole. Anxious to avoid getting rust in their hair, they all ducked and swerved (being careful not to tread on the deadly dentures) as they made their way into the room.

Ethel's windows weren't ordinary windows. They were stained glass, but they didn't show Bible characters like the windows you find in some churches. No, these colourful windows showed different foes that Charlie the Dog had defeated in the past. (Ethel was proud to be Charlie the Dog's maid.) These foes included: Four-Ton Fat Fraser from Fulham, Six-Ton Sick Sidney from Southgate, and Twelve-Ton Twisted Twacy from Twickenham. (Actually, her real name was Tracy, but Twacy sounds better next to Twickenham.) The trouble with these foes was that they were all too big to fit on a window, so Ethel had only shown their toenails. What a strange maid she was.

One more thing about Ethel's room: piled high on her bed were hundreds and thousands, and tens and hundreds of thousands, of colourful lids off the tops of Smartie tubes. The bed was sagging under their tremendous weight. Ethel threw them off when it was time to get to sleep, but she would always pile them back on top of it the next morning.

Did I say they were colourful? Well, they weren't very colourful at the moment. They all looked very pale as if they'd been out in the sun for a million years, give or take a millennium or two.

Ethel went as pale as the lids (the second time she'd gone pale today) when she saw what had happened to them.

'Oh my goodness,' she gasped. 'This is terrible. The time I took collecting all those lids, and now they're ruined.'

Charlie the Dog was puzzled. Surely the lids couldn't have faded as much as this in just a few hours—they were perfectly all right this morning. Something was definitely wrong here.

He was about to say so, when Ethel beat him to it.

'Something is definitely wrong here,' she continued gasping, and then she fumed: 'I'm so angry I could jump up and down.' Which she did.

Thump! went the floorboards after her first jump.

Thump! went the floorboards after her second jump.

Thump! repeated the floorboards after her third jump. (This was getting boring.)

And then, for a change, the floorboards went *Crruuunch!* after her fourth and final jump. Not only that, everyone in Ethel's room went 'Waaaahh!' as they descended through the floor and landed with more *Thump!*s in the living room below, surrounded by dust, broken floorboards, snapping dentures, thousands of Smartie lids and transparent birds or stars that flew in circles above their dazed and throbbing heads.

'Groan!' they all groaned.

'Groan! Atchsplishoo!' sneezed Belinda because she was allergic to dust.

But Charlie went: 'Groan! I'm going to find out what's going on here!' because he was a very determined detective.

He expertly stood up from the mess, waving away his annoying transparent bird, and investigated every square centimetre of the room, mumbling to himself, 'Got to find a clue as to why everything in my house seems to be broken or falling to bits.'

Not only did he explore every square centimetre. He also explored every triangular centimetre, and every round centimetre as well. But he didn't find a sausage...or any clues either.

'There must be a clue somewhere,' he reckoned, so he also investigated the kitchen, his study, his bedroom, the upstairs and downstairs toilets, and then the bathroom. Not long into investigating here, he screamed out: 'Ethel! Come quick! There's something here that you need to see!' This sounded pretty serious.

Ethel obediently raced up the stairs (after waving away her annoying transparent star), and joined her boss in the bathroom.

'What is it, sir?' she said after catching her breath. 'What do you...*oh.*' Ethel went paler than she'd ever been before. Charlie was pale as well, but you couldn't tell because his skin was covered in thick poodle fur.

This is why they were both pale: Norman the robot, Ethel's beloved boyfriend, was lazing in a bath of motor oil (his favourite form of relaxation). Or at least, *some* of him was lazing in the bath—a leg, two of his fingers, and his nose. That was all that remained of him, and these seemed to be fading fast as well. There was a note on the floor next to the bath that Norman must have hastily written when he realised his terrible plight. One of his fingers contained an inbuilt biro, and he'd scribbled on a thick, man-size tissue.

Charlie picked up the note, with motor oil stains all over it, and gravely handed it to Ethel. He didn't read

144

it; that wouldn't be right. Ethel needed to see it first because she'd been the closest to Norman.

Sobbing, she gratefully took the note and managed to read Norman's final, untidy words through her tears:

Darling Ethel,
   Looks like I'm finally falling apart. My construction from the beans and marmalade mixture in your fridge* couldn't have been as stable as we thought. I'm sorry things had to end this way, but we all have to go sometime, don't we? I'll miss you.
   Yours for ever,
         Norman the robot

Ethel, naturally, took this news very badly. So badly that she couldn't move. Her eyes were fixed on that note, not reading any more—just in stunned disbelief. She didn't speak either. There was nothing really to say.

Charlie took it badly as well, but he reacted differently. At first he was as silent as Ethel. He was thinking.

Norman had only been around a couple of months, and now he was gone. Everything that made up Norman—his delightfully scatty personality; his dancing skills; the way he seemed to come alive whenever his beloved Ethel was around—was gone now, for ever, never to be seen again. But wasn't that the same with humans as well? Once you were gone that was it. So tragic. The only difference was that humans stuck around a few decades longer.

Charlie then remembered his recent experience in

---

* See *The Great Baked Bean Scheme* for details of this.

level three of the Death Ride beneath Loch Ness.* There he had confronted, with his good friend Agatha, the possibility of a universe with no reason or meaning. A staggeringly large accident of a universe, containing an insignificant race of tinier accidents known as humans who really didn't matter one jot (or even half a jot) in the cosmic scheme of things. For all the impact they were making on the universe, they might as well not be there at all.

But hadn't he discovered that this wasn't the case? That a loving God had created everything for a reason, especially humans, and that we were all special in his eyes? That didn't seem to be true at the moment. Charlie and Ethel had had their disagreements over the years, but he hated to see her suffer like this. And what about Agatha? Her untimely death had been so unfair. Couldn't God have prevented this from happening? After all, he *was* supposed to be all-powerful. He must be a pretty rotten person to allow things like this to happen—if he existed at all, that is.

Once Charlie's thinking was over, he shouted as loud as he could to make up for Ethel's total silence. He also waved his fist towards the ceiling, because God was probably somewhere up there in that direction.

'This isn't good enough, God!' he shouted. 'When I started following you I never expected any of this! Everything's supposed to be all right when you become a Christian, isn't it? You could have stopped the deaths of Agatha and Norman, couldn't you? You could stop *everyone's* death! So why don't you put an end to all this suffering?'

---

* Again, see *The Great Baked Bean Scheme.*

No answer came from the ceiling. Instead, Charlie could hear two people talking downstairs. He tiptoed out to the top of the stairs, and listened in on some of their conversation:

'...not working, Dilwyn. What's wrong with all these people? We look into each of their minds to find out where they most want to be—then we take them there. But something *always* goes wrong.'

'That's right, Corman. And this house here where Ethel lives is very nearly the final straw. Inbuilt into everything associated with these humans seems to be death, decay and incompleteness. The process we used to transport Ethel and her friends here must have just speeded up the decay.'

'Come on, Dilwyn. Time to try out yet another ideal habitat on one of these strange people. Maybe this time we'll...urk!'

Corman gasped 'Urk!' because he noticed Charlie the Dog sliding down the bannisters and heading straight for them.

Dilwyn gasped 'Urk!' as well when he saw what his colleague had been gasping about.

But it was Charlie's turn next to gasp 'Urk!' when Dilwyn and Corman quickly stepped out of the way and Charlie bashed against the bookshelf by the bottom of the stairs. *The Guinness Book of Records* for that year, most of *The Encyclopaedia Britannica*, and Ethel's complete *Beano* collection, including all the annuals and summer specials, came crashing down on top of Charlie's head.

'Urk!' he went (though he couldn't be heard very well beneath the mountain of literature), and more stars and birds flew in circles above his buried head.

Charlie's intention had been to capture these two talkers (who were dwarf-size green-skinned aliens on

147

rollerskates) and find out at last what they were up to. He'd recognised Corman's voice—the same voice they'd heard booming out at them before in the lift. Only this time the voice sounded quite weedy.

But Charlie the Dog had failed. The aliens quickly tapped the floor with the tips of their rollerskates (activating some special controls), and before you could say, 'Special New Menacer Mike—makes your voice sound more menacing than it actually is—ideal for scaring away charging alien hordes or intimidating your captives,' their surroundings totally changed.

Charlie, minus the books and valuable comics, but still lying dazed on the floor, was now in some sort of giant mirror maze, lit by fluorescent lighting that seemed to stretch out into infinity (and maybe even further). Standing behind him was the Fiendish Fish Finger, embarrassed because he'd been standing behind the bookshelf and now he had nowhere to hide.

'Coo. What's 'appened 'ere?' he wondered, and he quickly ran behind a mirror (or was it a pane of glass?) before anyone could catch him again and stop him from jumping out from behind things and scaring people. The aliens in front of Charlie fled as well, but in the opposite direction on their rollerskates.

Pretty soon Charlie seemed to be the only person in the maze. All he could see were loads of his reflections looking back at him. What should he do now? Carry on recovering from all those books landing on him, that's what! And he grunted and groaned and grunted even more as he continued lying dazed on the ground.

But then he remembered that Norman had died, and that it was probably the fault of those aliens. Deep, powerful anger surged through his body, along with loads of energy. He had a fresh determination now to see justice done, and he jumped up quickly, pounded his fists against one of the mirrors to express some of that anger, then shouted out: 'I'm coming to get you!'

Would justice be done? *Would* Charlie get to those aliens? Only if he managed to find his way round this mirror maze....

9

Mirror Madness:
The Ideal World of the Fiendish Fish Finger

If Charlie and the others were ever to escape their strange predicament, it wouldn't be because of those helping in the foyer of the ACME Peace Corporation building.

As a matter of fact, they weren't helping at all. Remember the firemen and electricians had decided to say silly things and pull funny faces in the background while the BBC camera crew shot their news report? Well, things had escalated somewhat since then.

First, they'd progressed to pulling *each other's* faces and *shouting* silly things.

Then they progressed to singing old music hall numbers in ridiculously high pitched voices while performing energetic jigs. (This would make a great feature on Esther Rantzen's *That's Life*.)

Finally, the situation in the foyer had deteriorated into a chaotic free-for-all. Some in there were still singing and jigging. Others were performing their favourite party tricks: rippling their stomachs, playing tunes through their noses, or cleverly bending their double-jointed knees, elbows or finger joints in all sorts of weird and impossible directions. And dozens of people had joined them from outside, desperate to flee from the misery of un-Happy Hour. Some of these newcomers pretended to be monkeys and picked imaginary fleas off everyone. Others did energetic gymnastics, such as cartwheels or mid-air somersaults, smashed painfully into each other, then picked themselves up off the floor and started all over again. The remainder sprayed everyone with thick white foam from the fire extinguishers placed at strategic points around the foyer.

The cameraman and producer were loving every second of this as they faithfully shot everything that went on around them. They could sell their strange footage to TV stations around the world, and make a fortune. Honestly, the things some people would do to get on telly!

The only person in the foyer who wasn't enjoying himself was Derek Bowtie, the television reporter, who sat in one corner with his head in his hands.

'I wish I'd never suggested that everyone mess around behind me,' he wailed, tears shooting out of his eyes faster than the foam was spurting from the fire extinguishers. 'I didn't think things would get this silly. I'll never be taken seriously as a TV reporter again!'

If he was lucky, he reckoned, the BBC may still keep him on as an announcer for the Open University. Failing this, they might just let him be the person who goes 'Beeeeeeeep!' late at night, so that you wake up and turn your telly off before going up to bed.

If only Charlie and the others would come back, he wished, so that everyone would finally stop messing around. Maybe then his ordeal would be over.

But Charlie and the others were going through ordeals of their own—especially Charlie the Dog. This maze was terrible. Tall mirrors everywhere, joined by their sides to make hundreds of short twisting corridors that twisted in every direction corridors *can* twist (and sometimes in directions they *can't* twist as well). To make matters worse, clear panes of toughened glass were sometimes placed at the ends of corridors. If Charlie walked too quickly, he would bash straight into them because he couldn't see that they were there. His nose got bashed the most, and that was why he was now talking funny.

'Dis is codfusid,' he said (which meant, 'This is confusing.'). 'I'b beed here ted bidutes, ad I still habd't foud eddywod else' (which meant...oh never mind—it'll take too long to explain).

Charlie knew for a fact that the Fiendish Fish Finger was here—as well as those two aliens, if they hadn't beamed back to wherever they came from, that is. But something told Charlie that from now on they'd want to observe their dirty work from ground level so that they could figure out why they hadn't been having much success.

Charlie couldn't figure out why *he* hadn't been having any success. He'd covered hundreds of square metres in the last half-hour, yet hadn't come even remotely close to finding anyone else. How big exactly was this maze? Maybe he'd been going round in circles.

'Baybe I'b beed go-id roud id circles,' he said.

But then he said, 'By good-dess, it's Ethew!' (which means—yes, you've got it—'My goodness, it's Ethel!'). He could see her at the other end of the corridor, walking in his direction.

Ethel was still upset about Norman (she would be upset for a long time, naturally), and she was dragging

153

her gorilla feet along half-heartedly while looking miserably down at the ground. When she looked up and spied Charlie, however, she speeded up her pace. It was good to see someone again, especially her boss, and she desperately needed his shoulder to cry on.

Charlie speeded up his pace as well, as much as you can without actually running. It was comforting to have this confirmation that he *wasn't* alone in this maze.

'Ethew, it's you!' shouted Charlie.

'Sir, it's you!' Ethel shouted back.

Now they were running as fast as they could, their arms outstretched for a much-needed hug when they met.

Running was a *big* mistake! There was a hard pane of glass at the centre of the corridor, and they both ran into it at exactly the same time.

'Pwaah! Dot agaid!' screamed Charlie, as he fell ungracefully backwards.

'Yurgh! Didn't see that rotten glass there!' screamed Ethel, also falling backwards.

And then, to make matters even worse than before, the Fiendish Fish Finger jumped round a corner behind Charlie, shouted 'Boo!' while waving his arms in the air, then jumped right back to where he'd come from.

Seconds later, he jumped round the corner behind Ethel, shouted 'Boo!' again while waving his arms a bit more in the air, then disappeared back round that corner. Who knew when he would strike again?

Once he'd gone, more people appeared round those corners—but these people were friends. Towards Charlie ran X and Jonathan, with Esmerelda still in her bag. And towards Ethel sprinted Agent W and Belinda, not holding hands because their adventure in the jungle had made them realise how unsuited they were to each other. None of them had dust or bruises on them any more from their fall through Ethel's floor; the mess must have disappeared during the aliens' transportation process.

'Thank goodness, we found you!' X shouted to Charlie. 'We heard you screaming just now, so we headed immediately in your direction.'

Simultaneously W shouted exactly the same thing to Ethel, which was rather clever really. It sounded like stereo.

X and Jonathan picked Charlie up off the floor. W and Belinda picked Ethel up off the floor. And then the two groups looked at each other through the glass and wondered what they should do next. X, a natural leader, was the first to suggest their next course of action.

'Let's all head in that direction,' he said, pointing right (which, of course, was W's left), 'and hope that we somehow meet up. We'd better keep shouting so that we don't lose track of each other.'

The others agreed that this was a good plan (it was better than standing around doing nothing), and they gladly put it into action. Ethel didn't have the energy to shout, and neither did Charlie. But the others did a great job, screaming out pop songs, or rowdy football anthems, or *anything* to make themselves heard as they twisted and turned round dozens of different corners. Esmerelda couldn't shout, so she squirted water instead inside her bag.

Eventually the two groups did meet up, in a fun, long corridor that was made up of nothing but those distorted types of mirrors that you find at funfairs. Some of the mirrors made you look fat; some of them made you look thin. Some made you look tall; others made you look short. And there was one clever mirror that somehow made you look like a kangaroo.

The reunited group had a great time in this corridor, posing in front of the various mirrors and giggling as they did so. Even Ethel and Charlie began to perk up as they laughed at how ridiculous they both looked in front of their mirrors.

Jonathan liked the mirror that made him look taller. It helped him feel like a grown-up.

Belinda liked the mirror that made her look thinner. Her shape was perfectly okay, but she was convinced that she weighed much more than she should.

And W was particularly fascinated by the mirror that made him look like a kangaroo. He jumped up and down, and his kangaroo reflection jumped up and down with him. He scratched his nose with his hand, and the kangaroo reflection scratched its nose with its paw. He did a clever backward somersault, and the kangaroo reflection performed a clever backward somersault as well.

'Hey, this is brilliant!' said W, who'd never seen a mirror like it.

'Nah, it's not so brilliant!' replied the talking kangaroo. 'I've been stuck behind this pane of glass for ages, and I still can't find my way out of this maze.' Tears welled up in its eyes because it was ever so upset.

W was ever so upset as well. So that hadn't been his reflection after all. To try and cheer himself up, he looked round for another suitable mirror to have a giggle with—but suddenly he saw the Fiendish Fish Finger turning round a corner at his end of the corridor. Almost certainly, the Fish Finger was going to shout 'Boo!' really loudly while waving his arms in the air.

Which is exactly what he did. He shouted 'Boo!' really loudly and waved his arms in the air, and he was just about to disappear back round the corner when W challenged him: 'Come here and say that.'

Never one to turn down a challenge, the Fiendish Fish Finger stopped and said, 'Okay,' then changed his direction so that he was heading straight for Agent W.

But something was in his way. It was a giant pane of glass, and the Fiendish Fish Finger dashed into it at full speed with an ear-shattering *Pyoing!*, along with a heart-felt 'Yaaah!' He slumped to the floor, his squashed face sliding down the glass, which left thick, dripping grease stains.

'Groan,' mumbled the Fiendish Fish Finger, his head finally making contact with the floor. ''Ere oi wuz, finking this wuz the oideal place fer me—being able ter joomp round corners and scare poiple ter moi 'eart's content wivout 'em managing ter catch moi. But *oi'm* joost as loikely ter boomp inter fings as *they* are, aren't oi? This is useless.'

Yes, I know his accent is hard to understand. Basically, he said that he'd had enough of this mirror maze.

Just then Dilwyn and Corman rollerskated round the corner. They both looked more disappointed than ever.

'We've failed again,' moaned Corman, whizzing along on his skates. 'Only one person left now to try his ideal habitat on.'

'Let's do it then,' urged Dilwyn, 'and hope that finally someone is happy with their surroundings.'

They stopped skating just in front of the Fiendish Fish Finger; together they tapped the floor again with the tips of their rollerskates; and as they did so the mirror maze obediently faded, replaced by the familiar interior of the lift. It was quite a squeeze for everyone in there, especially since the now unconscious Fiendish Fish Finger was hogging most of the floor space. Dilwyn and Corman faced everyone else by the entrance.

Charlie the Dog was pleased that the two aliens were within strangling distance. He didn't feel particularly friendly towards them right now.

'How dare you cause Norman's death!' he screamed at them, his voice back to normal because he'd had time to recover. 'No one hurts my maid Ethel, do you hear me? No one!'

He reached his paws out to inflict extreme pain on them both (not something that Charlie normally did), but the aliens weren't worried. They knew that Charlie would very soon have other things on his mind—and they were right.

Just as Charlie was about to wrap his paws round Corman's tiny neck, the lift door opened, and facing him from outside was a very good friend of his. His *best* friend, in fact.

Charlie froze, his paws were millimetres from Corman. He gasped. He shuddered. His jaw dropped open in amazement. He closed his jaw so that it could drop open in amazement again—he was that amazed.

'You,' he said. 'It's you again. What are *you* doing here?'

'Beats me,' smiled his friend. 'Fancy a meal, Charlie? I'm absolutely famished!'

No one else existed now. Charlie dropped his paws and brushed past Dilwyn and Corman as he left the lift. He had joined his friend in the foyer of a fancy London restaurant, and they were waiting now to be seated.

He kissed his friend on the forehead, and she kissed him back, on his paw. This was brilliant— much too good to be true. The delightful Agatha Smethwick had somehow come back from the dead....

10

Charlie the Dog's Ideal World:
Heavens Above

'Zzzzzzz,' snored W and Belinda, Belinda's feminine head resting on W's firm shoulder.

'Zzzzzzz,' snored Jonathan and X, X's elderly head resting on Jonathan's not-quite-so-firm shoulder. (Esmerelda was snoring bubbles.)

'Zzzzzzz,' snored Dilwyn and Corman, Corman's alien head resting on Dilwyn's equally alien shoulder.

But Ethel snored 'Xxxxxxx,' instead because of her desire to be different. She was resting her head on both elbows, pushed cleverly together in the air in front of her. This wasn't very comfortable, but at least she was being original.

Why were they all sleepy? Because Charlie and Agatha hadn't stopped yacking since entering the restaurant three long hours ago. The Fiendish Fish Finger was unconscious as well, but for a different reason, remember?

The restaurant was quite posh (and, coincidentally, it was exactly the same restaurant that Charlie and Agatha had last eaten together in, fifteen years previously). The walls were decorated with high class, very expensive wallpaper; some of that wallpaper was obscured by high class and equally expensive plant life; high class waiters were tiptoeing round with trays full of high class grub; and high class music (none of that common top 40 racket) was blaring out of the restaurant's loudspeakers. Not that Charlie and Agatha were listening to any of it.

All were seated round a long wooden banquet table at the centre of this restaurant, except for the Fiendish Fish Finger who'd been placed underneath it. Charlie and Agatha were seated opposite each other at one end, staring at each other through the flickering flame of a tall-ish white candle. They hadn't spoken to anyone else during the whole three hours, not even their waiter, which is why they didn't yet have any food. The waiter had shouted at them, clapped his hands, and even pulled silly faces to try and get their attention—but the two of them hadn't noticed him in the slightest, they were that wrapped up in each other.

The first part of their conversation had dealt with Charlie's amazement—but also delight—that Agatha had come back from the dead.

'How on earth...? I mean, why, who, how...?' stuttered Charlie, finding it difficult to speak. He had a huge grin on his face, which didn't help much.

'Haven't a clue, Charlie,' Agatha answered, 'to *all* of your questions. But I do have to say, it *is* great to see you again.' Agatha was wearing the same smart dress she had on the last time she ate here, along with her impressive pearl necklace, shiny gold earrings and bright pink lipstick on her lips (where else?). There was her odd Zegan accent: unique but refreshing. And she smelt the same as well—wonderful!

Charlie did some thinking at this point, while continuing to grin, and he realised that he was the very last person from the group in the lift to have been transported somewhere by the aliens. This must be the place where he most wanted to be—he had many happy memories of his fun times with Agatha.

But how could the aliens have dragged Agatha back from heaven, if that was where she'd been? Maybe, as Charlie had suspected before, God had allowed this whole lift incident to happen so that they could all learn something.

Charlie's next question, naturally, involved Agatha's experiences in heaven. 'What's it like, Agatha?' he quizzed her. 'Up there, I mean, or wherever it is?'

'Hmm.' Agatha looked down, then up. She was thinking—this was a difficult question to answer. She looked down, then up, again. She was still thinking—how do you do justice to something so perfect, so brilliant, so *right*, using just a limited earthly language?

Eventually she smiled in a peaceful, contented sort of way and admitted, 'It's being with *him*, that's what it's all about.'

Charlie was surprised; this wasn't the answer he'd been expecting. He'd assumed that Agatha was going to describe some mind-blowing sights: endless stretches of green, rolling countryside; or breathtaking cities of gold, with shiny giant towers that pierced the pure blue sky. He also thought she would mention the joys of meeting old friends, or being reunited with long-gone members of her family.

But, no. The most important thing about heaven to Agatha seemed to be *'him'*.

'Being with him?' Charlie repeated.

'That's right, Charlie,' confirmed Agatha. 'Him.

163

Jesus. The man behind the whole enormous universe. He's great. It's like we were created to be with him, but unless we're actually *with* him we'll always feel incomplete.

'Being with him is like going for long walks with a loving father, who wants to know everything about you and cares for you a lot. It's like being with one of those schoolteachers who takes a special interest in you, and makes an effort to encourage you even when you're not doing that well. He's the perfect gentleman. I want to do everything for him. He's so…What's wrong, Charlie?'

Charlie the Dog looked pretty glum.

'You do believe, Charlie, don't you?' Agatha enquired.

'I…I'm not sure any more,' he answered. He had to be honest with his friend. 'I like what you're saying about heaven—I want that, believe me. But why can't it be that way on earth *right now?* Jesus still seems distant, even now I'm a Christian. I still feel incomplete. And there are so many bad things that happen in this life. It doesn't make any sense.'

Charlie sighed. Agatha smiled compassionately back at him.

Charlie sighed again. Agatha still smiled compassionately at him, with deep understanding in her eyes.

Then Charlie requested: 'Can we talk about something else? Hey, remember that time we dropped in on Plumthorpe's baked bean factory, and he…'

The rest of their conversation proceeded like this, as they remembered old times and laughed at all the funny experiences they'd been through together. Agatha was glad to talk like this; she was very fond of

Charlie. A shame that no one else was enjoying their animated conversation.

'Zzzzzzz!' continued just about everyone at the table, and Ethel continued with her unusual 'Xxxxxxx!'

Three hours into Charlie's and Agatha's nattering, the waiter made one last desperate attempt to attract their attention. (He'd never failed with customers before, and he was *very* frustrated.) After a number of panicked phone calls on the high class restaurant's pay phone, he had managed to persuade a number of groups of noise-makers to come and help him with his cause. All of these expert noise-makers were currently standing round Charlie's and Agatha's end of the table.

Convinced that his new effort would succeed, the waiter confidently blew into his whistle to signal that the first group of noise-makers should begin doing their thing. This group of eleven males and females of different ages and sizes, but with similarly-powered vocal cords, were members of the Cinemagoers Disruption Society (CDS for short), a secret and highly illegal organisation with branches throughout the land. Their aim: to disrupt all showings of films everywhere. You may have met one or two of them at your local cinema. They're always armed with something that rustles, like crisp or popcorn packets; they laugh in all the wrong places, especially if the film doesn't contain any humour; and they waffle on really loudly, even if there's no one sitting next to them to talk to.

The eleven were armed with more than their fair share of crisp and popcorn packets today, and once the waiter's whistle had blown they rustled them enthusiastically, getting mountains of popcorn and crisps on the floor. They also laughed hysterically at absolutely nothing (which they were experts at); and when they weren't laughing, they spouted out all sorts of nonsensical phrases, gabbling even louder than they did in the cinemas they visited.

Together they made quite a racket, and the other diners in the restaurant were annoyed at all this commotion. Charlie and Agatha weren't annoyed. They were still swapping humorous stories about their past, and hadn't noticed any of these strange new sounds.

'Grr,' grumbled the waiter, but he was determined to continue. He blew his whistle again so that the second group of noise-makers could add their sounds to the commotion. This second group, comprising ten tall men, wore nothing but striking, bright tartan: tartan kilts, tartan socks, tartan shirts, and tartan slippers as well because they wouldn't feel complete if something about their person wasn't made of striking, bright tartan. And they all held powerful tartan bagpipes, which was how they made their noise.

The whistle had gone, so they were energetically puffing and wheezing into their authentic Scottish bagpipes, blowing more powerfully than a force eight gale. What a din they made! Imagine three hundred screeching cats on heat; six hundred amateur violin players scratching away with their bows; and nine hundred dogs howling painfully because they can't stand the row from the three hundred cats and six hundred amateur violin players—and you'll get some idea of the appalling, ear-splitting wailing that came from the mere ten bagpipes. Add to this the continued rustling, laughing and spouting from the members of the Cinemagoers Disruption Society—and you'll understand why this high class London restaurant was shaking to its very foundations in sound. There was one almighty row in there.

166

But it still wasn't enough to get the attention of Charlie the Dog and Agatha.

'...or that factory head in Rochdale who insisted on demonstrating the Highland fling to us,' continued Charlie, rather appropriately considering the Scottish 'music' that was blaring out from behind him.

'Yes,' remembered Agatha, laughing, 'though "the Highland fiasco" would have been a more accurate name for it!'

'Titter. You're right!'

'Double grr!' grumbled the waiter, disappointed at their continued ignorance of all that was going on around them.

And those at the table continued snoring 'Zzzzzzz!' and 'Xxxxxx!' because even the monstrous row from the two groups of noise-makers hadn't managed to penetrate their deep and blissful sleep. They'd all been through a lot.

But the waiter wasn't going to give up just yet. He still had one more group of noise-makers up his sleeve. (Actually, they were standing just next to him.) He blew into his whistle for the third and final time, and while the eleven CDS members carried on disrupting, and the ten bagpipe players skilfully persisted in producing nothing that was tuneful whatsoever, the third group set about doing what they'd been asked here for.

Actually, they weren't a group—they were really a duo, on loan from a nearby circus, along with a high-powered cannon that they'd pushed all the way to the restaurant. The duo, dressed in dazzling yellow outfits that would blind you if you stared at them too long, were the Human Cannonball act at the circus, and they calmly took their places so that the third loud noise could be produced.

The braver member of the duo climbed feet-first into the barrel of the cannon, slipping all the way down so that none of him could be seen any more. And the chicken of the duo (yellow in more ways than one) lit a larger-than-life prop match so that he could set off the cannon.

He shook a bit when he brought the prop match down (he was nervous, poor chap), so the match kept missing its target at the back of the cannon. Eventually, though, he did hit target, and the cannon went 'BOOOOOMM!', hurling the brave human inside all the way across the restaurant. This was the loudest noise that had ever been heard inside this restaurant, and just about everyone stopped what they were doing in shock, even the bagpipe players and the members of the CDS.

Everyone round Charlie's and Agatha's table had woken up with a jump, as well as the Fiendish Fish Finger. He'd shot up from the ground, but bashed his head on the bottom of the table and fell back down unconscious again.

All the other diners in the restaurant had jumped up from their seats; and the waiter had jumped up as well because he hadn't expected the cannon to be quite so loud.

Charlie and Agatha didn't jump up—but they weren't talking either. They'd finally run out of memories to remind each other about.

It wasn't long before Charlie was yacking about something else, however. 'Well,' he said, smiling because he was enjoying himself immensely, 'since we can't get any service around here'—and he looked angrily round at this point—'we might as well head somewhere else. Fancy some burgers? We could take them away and eat them by the Thames.'

'Sounds good to me,' responded Agatha. 'I'm even more absolutely famished than before.'

They shook hands to show that they agreed this was a good idea, then stood up and headed for the exit, urging their colleagues at the table to join them.

'Grr, grr and *triple* grr,' fumed the waiter, totally fed up because Charlie and Agatha still hadn't noticed him after all his hard efforts. He snatched one of the bagpipes, and jumped up and down on it in total frustration. The bagpipes responded by howling deafeningly, and the noise-makers crowded round him, applauding with much admiration because he was making a worse noise than all of them put together.

Meanwhile, a diner in a far corner of the restaurant was summoning another waiter.

'Waiter! Waiter!' he called to the waiter (who else?). 'There's a human in my soup!' He wasn't lying: the dazed human cannonball had landed on his table.

The waiter eyed the human cannonball, thought for a moment, then wittily replied: 'Ha ha! Do you want a doggy bag for it, sir?' Well, the waiter thought it was witty, at least.

The human cannonball definitely didn't. He got up, angrily slapped the waiter across the cheek, then ran back over to his cannon so that he could climb fully inside. That was the only reason he put up with this job: when he was inside that cannon he felt completely safe from the world outside and all its many problems. What a shame that he always had to be shot out of it again.

'Beautiful, isn't it?'

'Yeah, brilliant, Charlie. Chomp!'

This was Charlie and Agatha, of course, and they

were leaning over the side of Waterloo Bridge, admiring the scenery. It was dark outside 'cause it was night-time, but Charlie preferred it that way. To him, there was no better place than the River Thames at night in London. The reassuring splashing of the water beneath them. The office blocks, or the historical buildings lit up all around them. The stars in the night sky twinkling down at them, or the moon brightly shining through the clouds. And the renewing sensation of life and busyness that you get when you're in the middle of a bustling city like this. Wonderful.

Charlie often came here after a hard day of detection, so that he could unwind or get things in perspective. Sometimes he would pray as well. This was the nearest thing he knew to heaven.

The second nearest thing was a fat, greasy hamburger, and he was greedily tucking in to one right now. So was Agatha, and that was why she'd 'Chomp!'ed a short while ago.

No one else was eating any hamburgers. All of Charlie's colleagues from the lift had had their fill back at the restaurant, and they were sitting cross-legged on the pavement, silently waiting for Charlie and Agatha to finish so that they could finally get back to their homes and recover. It had been a long, discouraging day for them. The Fiendish Fish Finger was still unconscious and was lying on the pavement between Dilwyn and Corman. These two aliens looked slightly less fed up than the others because it appeared that at last someone was pleased with the surroundings they'd been placed in.

The aliens, of course, were the owners of the invisible flying saucer still hovering above the ACME Peace Corporation building. Just why had they visited this planet in their saucer? Why had they captured this interesting combination of people in the lift? And why had they transported them all to different environments—some of them normal; some not quite so normal?

Conveniently, X asked the aliens these very same questions because he couldn't think of anything better to do while waiting for Charlie and Agatha.

'Just why have you visited this planet?' he started. 'Why did you capture this interesting combination of people in our lift?' he continued. 'And why did you transport us all to different environments—some of them normal; some not quite so normal?' he concluded.

Corman figured it was all right to answer X's questions. If X and the other earthlings didn't like his answers, and decided to express their dislike with certain forms of violence, all Dilwyn and Corman had to do was beam themselves up to the safety of their spaceship. The only reason they were down here was to observe first-hand their successes and failures in their final attempts at finding ideal habitats for people.

'To answer your first question,' started Corman, 'we visited *this* planet because we were impressed with how determined and hard-working your species seems to be.'

'Coo. Thank you,' said X, smiling because he appreciated this alien's compliment.

'To answer your second question,' continued Corman, 'we scanned many areas of this planet with our equipment, but felt that those who happened to be in the ACME Peace Corporation lift at that time were the prime specimens of your race.' (He must have had faulty equipment.)

'Coo. Thank you again,' said X, smiling even more

because he'd never been considered a prime specimen of the human race before.

'And to answer your third question,' concluded Corman, 'our aim is to transport the entire human race to one of our moons on the other side of the galaxy. You are going to be our slaves and do lots of mining for us. We wanted to find an ideal habitat where you would all feel at home and so wouldn't complain too much. We will construct this habitat on our moon.'

'Coo. Thank you even more,' said X, smiling because what Corman had just said hadn't sunk in yet. But when he finally realised the awfulness of what had been spoken, he stood up and thundered, 'You can't do that! The human race isn't yours for the taking! I've a good mind to ...!'

Dilwyn and Corman stood up as well, getting ready to tap the tips of their rollerskates on the ground so that they'd be beamed back up to their ship and so wouldn't be throttled by X. But they weren't in danger any more. X had stopped in mid-sentence, distracted because he saw that Charlie and Agatha had finished eating their burgers and were turning away from the river. Maybe, he prayed, they'd finished at last.

Charlie the Dog was a super-skilled detective, trained to notice every small detail that went on around him so that he could more effectively solve all his cases. But, unusually for him, he hadn't heard a word of X's and Corman's conversation. He'd been too wrapped up in the Thames and Agatha. (No one else had heard the conversation either; *they'd* been too wrapped up in their own misery.) Charlie and Agatha hadn't exchanged many words on this bridge. For Charlie, just being with his friend again and enjoying the scenery and junk food was enough.

But now Agatha seemed uncomfortable.

'What's wrong, Agatha?' Charlie asked her, deeply concerned. 'Is it the burger you ate? I know it was a bit greasy.'

'No, no, it's not the burger,' Agatha assured him, looking more miserable by the second. 'It was delicious, believe me.'

'Is it being out here at night?' Charlie wondered. 'I know most people prefer the daytime. Is it...?'

Agatha cut him short. 'And it's not that either,' she insisted. 'It's great here. The lights. The water. Everything.'

Insecure Charlie looked down at the ground. 'Then it's me, isn't it? I've waffled on too much this evening, haven't I? Sorry about that. I've bored you, and I want to...'

Agatha smiled and gently slapped him on the cheek. 'Rubbish, Charlie,' she rebuked him. 'It's brilliant being with you—honest. Don't *ever* think that I'm bored with you.' The smile disappeared, and her sweet but sad expression returned.

'Then what is it?' Charlie demanded. 'What could possibly be the matter?'

'It's cold,' Agatha answered. 'Terribly, terribly cold.'

'Huh?' Charlie didn't understand her. It was cool outside, admittedly, but far from freezing. And Agatha was tightly wrapped up in her thick coat that she'd retrieved from the restaurant's cloakroom. What was she talking about?

'I don't know what you mean,' admitted Charlie, genuinely wanting to understand. 'Why do you say it's cold?'

'Not *physically* cold, Charlie,' Agatha explained, her voice somewhat strained because of her pain. 'It's *spiritually* cold.'

Charlie didn't respond. He obviously didn't understand.

Agatha saw his puzzled look, and tried to make things clearer. 'There with *him*, it's just so right. It's the way it was always meant to be. But here, this earth, it's incomplete, it's running down. This earth is okay, but there's so much more. I guess people get so used to the way things are, it never even occurs to them that there's a much better place.'

'So... so what does that have to do with you being cold?' asked Charlie.

This was simple to answer. 'Once you've seen things the way they're *supposed* to be—experienced it—anything else leaves you dissatisfied. I used to be quite happy in my ignorance while living in this universe, but now that I've been with him—well, the contrast is so strong.'

'Like watching on a colour TV after years of black and white,' suggested Charlie. 'You never want to go back to the black and white.'

'Yes, something like that,' responded Agatha, half-heartedly. She stared at her friend and lifted a hand to wave goodbye. 'I must be off now,' she announced. 'You'll always be special to me, Charlie. It was brilliant seeing you again, and that was why it took me so long to notice the cold. But now...' She was fading away. '...now I need to go home.'

'No, no, don't go!' Charlie protested, reaching out to her. 'I need you here, desperately. We work well together. We could help each other. We...' But she was gone. Charlie had reached out to grab nothing but air. It suddenly seemed to have got an awful lot colder for him as well. This was the third time he had lost Agatha, and each time their parting became unbearably more difficult.

Charlie couldn't handle facing his colleagues. He leaned over the side of the bridge again, hoping that they wouldn't see the pained expression on his face.

Sensing that things had come to an end, Dilwyn and Corman stood back up, lifting the still unconscious Fiendish Fish Finger as they did so. (Dilwyn took the arms, and Corman had the legs.)

'Well, that's it then,' announced Dilwyn, jubilantly, ready to tap the ground with his rollerskates again so that everyone could return to the lift. 'Our task is over. All we have to do now is make sure the whole of our moon looks like this River Thames at night.'

Charlie mumbled something then. Dilwyn and Corman didn't quite hear him.

'What was that?' requested Corman, and Charlie responded by spinning round and snapping at him. His tolerance level was low.

'It's *not* the River Thames!' he screamed. 'Not the Thames at all!' he insisted. How dare this alien not fully understand him. 'It's Agatha! That's where I want to be: where Agatha is!'

This was a dangerous thing to say when the aliens' 'ideal habitat' machinery was still in operation. If Charlie felt at home somewhere, he would be immediately transported there. Since he wanted to be with Agatha, he suddenly found himself where she was— and we all know where that is, don't we? The others found themselves there as well. Maybe the aliens' machinery had been given a divine boost to help them all get there.

What was it like—all sweetness and beauty? Not at all—it was *painful*. Everyone felt as if they were burning. Extreme heat surrounded them. They couldn't see because of the intense, bright light. It was like they

175

were in the centre of the most ferocious of fires. Awful!

But then the pain stopped. Everyone felt clean. And all of the sadness and disillusionment that they had gone through today didn't matter any more. That was because they knew, with no doubts whatsoever, that all the things that happen in this world are part of an immense, complex plan where everything will turn out all right in the end. Even the bad things are there for a reason—not meaningless in the slightest.

The fire had gone, but the heat was still there—though it was a soothing heat now rather than a ferocious one. And the light was still bright—but it was bathing and gentle rather than blinding.

Not that anyone was seeing properly. Everything was blurred for them because of the tears in their eyes. They were tears of relief at being released at last from all the pain and hurts and guilt that they'd built up over the years. They were tears of joy at ending up in this place that communicated 'home at last'—making earth, even the really awe-inspiring parts of it, seem nothing more than a shabby waiting place for here. And they were tears of shame—shame that they hadn't understood sooner how wonderful, how awesome, how brilliant, this person behind the whole of creation is, and how wide and deep is his love. They felt him there so strongly that they weren't aware of anything or anyone else, not even Agatha Smethwick.

All were on their knees before him, and each in turn confessed that he was 'Lord...', realising who it was that was in front of them. Each, that is, except for two aliens and a Fiendish Fish Finger.

Dilwyn and Corman had been freaked out by this fire experience, and they'd both tapped their roller-skates quickly so that they could get straight back to their spaceship. They were still holding the Fiendish Fish Finger, so he was beamed back with them. If only they'd stayed a bit longer; some people just don't like being confronted with how dirty and rotten they are.

Charlie didn't notice that these three had disappeared. All he cared about at the moment was getting closer to this person who'd been so kind to him, especially after that trouble a while back with the Clothes Line Snatcher. Charlie was the only one in the group to stand up (the others couldn't bear looking at this person), and he boldly walked towards him. The person's features couldn't be seen very well because of the strong, white light. All Charlie knew was that he was smiling, and he could feel that smile penetrating deep within his soul.

Charlie smiled back at him, while still walking closer. 'You tricked me, didn't you?' he laughed. 'You knew this was going to happen. You let Agatha disappear down there as bait for me. The only reason I wanted to come here was to be with her, but now that I'm here... well, I didn't realise it but *you're* the person I really want to be with.'

The man didn't confirm this. He just continued smiling, with deep understanding in his eyes.

Charlie reached out to touch him, just like he'd reached to touch Agatha. When he did he felt incredible; felt whole again; felt as if the short time he'd been a Christian he'd only been able to view this person through dark sunglasses, but now could see him as if his shades were off. If only Charlie had been able to see him that clearly on earth, maybe he wouldn't have grumbled at him so much. Everything made perfect sense now. It...

It had got an awful lot colder. That was because Charlie and his colleagues were back in the lift, and

Charlie was now touching the cold metallic doors. Charlie couldn't talk for a while, and neither could his colleagues. What *could* they say?

Eventually, though, Charlie went, 'Phew—that was—wow—I mean—you know—cor.' As you can see, meeting the all-powerful person behind everything—and, more amazing than that, knowing that he actually *liked* you—was, well, difficult to put into words.

The others in the lift were equally blown away, though they didn't yet share Charlie's assurance that this person liked *them*. They couldn't look into his eyes back there because they knew they hadn't made their peace with him yet. They wanted to put that right as soon as possible, though. They were determined to get to know him better.

All carried on like Charlie for a few minutes, saying nothing but 'Wow' and 'My goodness' and other such utterances while marvelling at how wonderful heaven had been. But X was the first to bring them down to earth again (typical) by observing: 'I see our alien friends and that Fish Finger aren't with us any more.'

'You're right,' confirmed Charlie, looking round the lift. He thought for a few seconds, then concluded: 'They must have scarpered when we found ourselves in heaven, and taken the Fiendish Fish Finger with them for some reason. Good riddance too, I say. Let's just hope that horrible burning gave them such a fright that they'll never bother with this planet ever again.' (Charlie's hope was right: they didn't dare come back to earth.)

He turned back round to face the doors. 'Now how do we get out of this thing?'

'Easy,' said Ethel, and she happily pressed the

'DOORS OPEN' button for the second time that day. Like before, the button worked. Fantastic.

Charlie and the others were free now...for ever.

11

The Real World Revisited

The foyer of the ACME Peace Corporation building was still alive with strange activity. People were singing and jigging, and performing their favourite party tricks, *and* pretending to be monkeys, *and* cleverly doing energetic gymnastics in the limited space available, *and* spraying thick white foam all over the place from the dozen-or-so fire extinguishers that used to be on the walls. Not only that, even more people had poured in from outside, performing crazier stunts than the others to cheer themselves up. You see, to those not in the lift it appeared that Charlie and the others had only been away for slightly more than half an hour. This meant that un-Happy Hour was still in effect, and therefore people still wanted to hide in the foyer to escape all the misery.

Even Derek Bowtie had joined in with the party-trick crowd (lying on the ground while expertly rippling ten pence pieces along his stomach) because he'd figured, 'If you can't beat them, join them.' And the cameraman and producer were still eagerly shooting everything in sight. They had more material on tape now than they knew what to do with.

Everyone was so engrossed in what they were

doing that when the lift doors finally reopened and Charlie the Dog stepped out, no one noticed. They didn't even notice X, Ethel, W, Belinda, and Jonathan with Esmerelda in her bag, when they followed Charlie into the foyer.

X was appalled at the chaos all around him. After all, he *was* the head of ACME, and he liked to see order in his building—not utter madness like this. 'What on *earth* is going on here?' he wondered really loudly so that he could be heard above the phenomenal din.

'Probably something to do with un-Happy Hour,' theorised Charlie, also loudly so that X could hear him.

'Oh, that stupid thing,' grumbled X. 'I'd forgotten about that. We can't have been gone that long, then, if it's still going on.'

Charlie agreed. 'You must be right.'

They surveyed the chaos a bit more as the lift doors closed behind them, then Jonathan, bright-eyed, shouted: 'So, what now, Mr Charlie the Dog? How can we possibly top what we've just been through?'

Charlie turned and smiled at him. 'We're never going to top *that*, young Jonathan,' he shouted back. 'How can you beat a meeting with the Almighty? I reckon, though, that a celebration is in order—for seeing the earth saved from those despicable aliens, but mainly for being with *him*. I suggest a slap-up feast at the next best thing to heaven—when the lovely Agatha's not around, that is—Greasy Joe's Caff round the corner!'

Agent W cheered. He loved greasy food. Belinda affectionately squeezed his hand because she was glad that he was pleased. She hoped that they could still be friends.

X looked pleased as well, a surprising reaction considering his previous feelings towards Greasy Joe's. Perhaps the events of today had softened him up. The only person whose smile was half-hearted was Ethel. Charlie noticed this and asked her what was wrong.

'It's Norman, sir,' she said. 'Heaven was great, and I know that *he* means good for everything. But... well, do robots end up in heaven?'

Charlie couldn't answer this, so he just gave Ethel a hug to show her that he felt for her. Then he urged everyone: 'Come on, let's head round the corner. I'm famished.'

'Me too,' said Agent W—and everyone else was as well, including Esmerelda. She hoped that Joe served ultra-greasy goldfish food.

As the seven of them headed happily out of the foyer, all (except Esmerelda) cheerfully announced to those around them that: no one had to be so miserable any more; God was in charge and could be trusted; they could have the hope of heaven in their lives if they promised to live for Jesus; and also, they could celebrate this hope right now by joining them in a greasy, fattening fry-up at Joe's. Yum.

The hope of heaven, eh? Fantastic! You'd think that everyone would want to go for this, wouldn't you? But only a few from the foyer marched out with Charlie and the gang. Those remaining either couldn't believe ('Sounds much too good to be true'), or didn't fancy the idea of handing their lives over to someone, preferring instead to do things their way even though they weren't doing that well. If only they knew how great God is, and what they were missing out on. Sad really, isn't it?

The reaction was the same on the streets outside, from those still staring miserably at each other—in cars or through shop windows—or crying hysterically because of un-Happy Hour.

'You don't have to be miserable!' was the message they were told enthusiastically, but again only a handful joined Charlie's parade on the trek to Greasy Joe's Caff. The handful looked pretty happy, though. It was great that they'd found the answer.

Once this group reached the café, Charlie kicked the door open (just like cowboys in films when they enter the local saloon) and loudly ordered: 'Twenty of the greasiest meals on your menu, please, Joe.'

Things had calmed down somewhat since X and Charlie had last been in here. (Had it really been less than an hour ago?) No one was swinging from light fittings in the ceiling any more, or violently squirting vinegar or tomato ketchup at each other. They must have run out of energy.

But they hadn't run out of misery. They were sitting glumly at their messy tables, looking glumly at the walls or floor or ceiling, while sighing really glumly and trying to look more glum than anyone else around them. In short, they were pretty glum.

Except for one of Joe's customers. He wasn't blue like the others. He was silver because he was made of strong alien metal. His name was Norman the robot, and he was overjoyed to see his darling Ethel walking through the door. Ethel was just as overjoyed to see him, and they ran towards each other in pretend slow motion, just like those romantic bits in films.

Charlie wondered why they were running so slowly, but then he shrugged his shoulders. He was used to his maid's and the robot's strange behaviour. But how could Norman still be alive?

'Hello, Norman. How can you still be alive?' he

asked Norman, still running towards Ethel. (He was ever so slow.)

Norman replied: 'Iiiiiii hoooooonesssssstlyyyyyy dooooooon't...' talking really slowly and low to go with the speed of his running. He didn't finish his sentence. He crashed into Ethel. Ethel crashed into him. And they both fell to the ground in slow motion, which was ever so clever—clutching their heads because they were in pain.

Once on the ground, they returned to normal speed. Norman jumped up and finished answering Charlie's question: '...know.' Wasn't worth waiting for really, was it? But then he continued: 'I faded away in the bathtub, but the next thing I knew I was back to normal again in the motor oil. Don't know how it happened. All I know is I was desperate to tell Ethel I was okay, so I got on the train to where I thought I might find her.'

'Hmm,' said Charlie, resting his chin on his fist, which is what all world-famous poodle detectives do when they're thoughtful. 'Maybe when the aliens disappeared, everything in my house returned to normal. Good, that also means that Ethel's Smartie tube lids are colourful again.'

Norman didn't hear Charlie's spoken thoughts. He had picked Ethel up, hugged her really tightly, and was now doing the tango with her round the café. They were cleverly avoiding the splodges of ketchup, puddles of vinegar, and heaps of salt and pepper on the floor.

Ethel was thoroughly enjoying herself. 'I'm thoroughly enjoying myself,' she cleverly managed to announce while doing this energetic dance. Then she added, smiling like she'd never smiled before: 'This has been the very best day of my life!'

Charlie was pleased. It was great to see his maid so happy. Then he remembered the doubts he'd expressed this morning about his future career at the ACME Peace Corporation. He realised that, for some reason, these doubts didn't exist any more.

'How strange.'

Just to make sure, Charlie prayed a short, quiet prayer towards the ceiling: 'What should I do about the future?'

Almost immediately, his answer came back in the form of a loud but gentle thought in his head: 'You're a great detective, Charlie. I made you that way.' There was no more to the answer than that, but it was more than enough.

So that was it, then. God wanted him to carry on being the best detective he could. That was what he was made for. Sounded good to him. And somehow now he felt that he could cope.

He turned to X and whispered in his ear: 'I'm staying at ACME, X. Looks like you've got me for at least a few more years.'

'Really?'

X smiled.

X grinned.

X laughed.

Then X came out with an ear-splitting 'Yaaahoooo!' because he was totally overjoyed. He picked up one of the few plastic ketchup containers that still had ketchup in it, and happily squirted it at Charlie the Dog to show him how pleased he was that he was staying.

Charlie grabbed a similar container with a small amount of vinegar in it, and proceeded to squirt it at his boss because he too was thrilled with his decision.

Belinda was happy. She was chatting up Greasy Joe because she found him quite cuddly.

Agent W couldn't be more content. He was polishing off everyone's meals that they hadn't finished because of un-Happy Hour.

Jonathan was sprinkling loads of greasy goldfish food in Esmerelda's bag, smiling because he'd grown quite fond of her during their adventures in the lift. He promised to buy her a large glass tank as soon as they got back home, something that Esmerelda was extremely pleased to hear.

And the others who'd come into the café with Charlie had formed themselves into whatever a barbershop quartet would be called if it had fourteen people in it instead of just four. They had laid hankies across their arms instead of barbershop towels, and they were tunefully singing cheery songs of joy, hope and happiness because that was how they felt.

Their songs were cheering all the glum customers up.

Looked like it was a really happy ending for Charlie and the others, but it was a different story for the aliens in their spaceship as they zoomed back to their planet as fast as they were able.

One: they'd failed in their mission.

And two: that pesky fish finger they'd brought with them was scaring them all around the ship.

'Boo!' he screamed for the three-hundredth time on this journey, this time jumping out from the engineering section then jumping back inside.

'Aaahh!' screamed Dilwyn and Corman, jumping up, then dashing inside the engineering section so that they could capture this nuisance and beam him as far away as possible. But he'd disappeared from engineering before they'd even passed through the entrance. He was much too quick and slippery for them. This could go on for ever.

If only those aliens had stayed with Jesus a bit longer. Maybe things would have turned out better for them.

It was good to see Charlie the Dog happy again.

Oodles Of Poodles

by Andrew Wooding

When *Dickie Dustbin* met a genie in a coke can, he knew that life was going to change. *But not this much...*

Enter one *Charlie Digestives*, world-renowned poodle detective, in search of the dreaded *Clothes Line Snatcher*, who has even more wicked designs on the universe than whipping socks off clothes lines. Will *Charlie* catch up with the fiend before it's *too late for all life?* Will the real *Dickie* triumph over the vile life-size photocopy of himself *and* discover what true love is all about?

Phoenix

Published by Kingsway

The Great Baked Bean Scheme

by Andrew Wooding

Charlie the amazing poodle detective is brave and fearless. At least, he thought he was.

But when his long-lost friend **Agatha** returns, **Charlie** is on the trail of a dastardly plot to take over the universe using the earth's rich supply of baked beans. Before him lies the triple horror of the Death Ride, where he has to face the ultimate fear. No one has survived before...

 *Phoenix*
Published by Kingsway